OWLISH

Also by Dorothy Tse in English

Snow and Shadow

OWLISH

A NOVEL

Dorothy Tse

Translated from the Chinese by Natascha Bruce

Graywolf Press

This publication is made possible, in part, by the voters of Minnesota through a Minnesota State Arts Board Operating Support grant, thanks to a legislative appropriation from the arts and cultural heritage fund. Significant support has also been provided by the McKnight Foundation, the Amazon Literary Partnership, and other generous contributions from foundations, corporations, and individuals. To these organizations and individuals we offer our heartfelt thanks.

The author and translator would additionally like to express their gratitude to the PEN/Heim translation grant and residencies at the Leeds Centre for New Chinese Writing and the Art Omi Translation Lab for their support of the translation of *Owlish*.

An excerpt from this book first appeared in *Denver Quarterly*, *Granta*, and *Two Lines*.

Published by Graywolf Press
212 Third Avenue North, Suite 485
Minneapolis, Minnesota 55401

www.graywolfpress.org

Published in the United States of America

ISBN 978-1-64445-235-6 (paperback)
ISBN 978-1-64445-236-3 (ebook)

2 4 6 8 9 7 5 3 1
First Graywolf Printing, 2023

Library of Congress Control Number: 2022946115

Cover design: Kapo Ng

Cover art: Sam Chung

OWLISH

0

Love is blind, as the saying goes. Although, in the case of Professor Q, it would be more accurate to say that love had rearranged his vision.

Which would explain why, on that gluey winter afternoon, with the air weighing heavily on his brain, when Professor Q gazed as usual through the stainless steel grille over his narrow little window, he didn't see the ocean. Nor did he note the emergence of a razor-sharp sun, slicing the water into thousands of glassy splinters, or the continued existence of the bright, soldierly dredgers that were always working in the bay, their mechanical arms flexing up and down into the seabed. No, what Professor Q saw was the city he had lived in for many years swelling into a head, then slowly rotating to show him its other face.

He didn't notice this face at first. He was preoccupied by thoughts of a five-digit number, which was linked somehow to an old friend of his. The two of them had once been very close but now the friend seemed shadowy and small, like a cockroach hidden in a dark corner of his memory, feebly waving its antennae. He extended a finger and carefully tapped the number into the keypad of his new smartphone. His hand was tensed, as though opening a safe. No: as though setting the code on a bomb. It couldn't be a phone number, he thought. If it ever had been, it would be disconnected by now; it was three digits shorter than the ones currently used in Nevers.

And yet, when he pushed the button to dial, the call connected, making his heart thump wildly.

'So, you remember me at last!'

A laugh sounded down the line. The voice was so distant and shady, so full of echoes, it could have been coming from inside a damp cave. After the laugh, the head outside the window finished its turn towards Professor Q. Then he saw a pair of long, slender, birdlike eyes, a mouth that was widening into a grin, and a pile of messy hair. Owlish! Could this really be Owlish? How could he have forgotten him for all this time?

'I'm in a spot of trouble.'

As he spoke, Professor Q realized he sounded almost cheerful. He was reconnecting with an old friend and, already, he felt as though his situation was starting to improve. He was half a century old, embroiled in his very first extramarital affair, and everything suddenly seemed much less terrible than he'd been imagining. His bland, uneventful life finally contained something worth talking about. This was cause for celebration, surely? He poured the tale of his twilight romance into the phone, after which Owlish chuckled heartily, then suggested paths that had never before occurred to the professor.

'What you need is a love nest.'

A love nest? Owlish's words appeared in Professor Q's mind as a map. The lines and contours of this map resembled the Nevers he knew, except many of the roads and districts had names he hadn't heard before. When he thought of Nevers, it was all sunshine, dusty glass, and the smell of banknotes, but the place Owlish described was heavy metals, damp cloth, the scent of plastic. He gripped his phone and looked out at the sea, partially hidden behind his dark green curtain. His old friend's face was blurry again. The sunlight bouncing off the water turned vicious and stabbed at his eyes, forcing them into a squint.

'This is the place. All those secrets you've been storing up for all these years, now there's a home for them. Not just for your lover; for anything you need to keep quiet. Cram it all in!'

Professor Q mouthed the address Owlish gave him, feeling as though it was in a foreign language, the words just meaningless sounds. He pulled a pen without a cap from his pen pot and jotted the sounds on a home improvement magazine, in the corner of an advertisement for watches. After ending the call, he realized the dried-up ballpoint had failed to leave any ink on the paper, although the grooves of his handwriting were there, passing right through the glossy page and appearing as raised outlines on the other side. Running his callused fingers over the surface felt intensely erotic.

1

The moment it all started can be traced back to Professor Q's fiftieth birthday. He was strolling along an antiques market on Valeria
Island when a peculiar, birdlike expression flitted across his face.
No one with him at the time had noticed, but his palms were instantly sweaty and his whole body began to tremble.

The early autumn leaves were dry and wilting, just starting to
curl in on themselves. Professor Q and his companions had been
out clam-digging and were draped in lacklustre windbreakers,
their hair full of the smell of salt. For the past few years they had
been getting together at least once a month, going for hikes in the
winding Nevers mountain ranges, or for walks along its meandering coastline, or, as on this particular day, on boat trips to its tiny
outlying islands and then back again, to Valeria Island city centre. Out on the water that morning, the head-on wind had engulfed them the same way the fog smothered the view, erasing
them from the city's memory. But when the filthy ocean foam had
pushed their boat back into Valeria Harbour, back towards the
towering office blocks and their shimmering, mirrored façades,
they were confronted once again with evidence of their diminishing physical forms. And rather than being alarmed by the sight of
the ageing voyagers pressing in from the other side of the glass,
they felt a strange kind of relief. They were boatmen on the verge

of accomplishing their mission. Just a little longer, and they would be safely delivered to the other shore.

Most of the group had lived all their lives in this coastal territory called Nevers, located to the south of Ksana. Nevers had been built up by the kingdom of Valeria and ruled by her for over a hundred years, developing first on Valeria Island and then expanding to the Ksanese peninsula across the harbour. Nowadays, the city was looking well past its prime. Skyscrapers thrust upwards like lethal weapons and, at fixed times every evening, a light show started up on both sides of the harbour, laser beams strafing the water and blinding passers-by. The group left their boat and headed towards the western side of Valeria Island, leaving behind the high-rises and entering the city's maze-like alleys where there were still shophouses even older than they were. The shopfronts were narrow, displaying a few pine coffins or stacked bamboo rocking chairs and baskets, with upstairs floors that extended over the street, darkened windows tightly closed. Now and then someone might be glimpsed shuffling behind the glass, but, then again, perhaps it was just the reflection of a drifting cloud.

After the blond-haired, blue-eyed Valerian colonizers occupied the central zone of Valeria Island, one of their first actions was to lay down a road named after their empress. Before long, barracks, opium depots, dance halls, and bars sprang up along both sides. When thousands of Ksanese came fleeing the war inland, bringing with them only what they could carry, they gathered to the west of these developments, where they cobbled together badly ventilated, two- or three-storey shophouses. They raised animals and peddled goods on the ground floors, and used wooden boards to divide the cramped upper storeys into even tinier spaces, which they then rented out. These houses were so dark and hot that some residents moved their kitchens outside and squatted by the road to cook, hawking food to passers-by. Early in the morning, congee sellers would cross paths with night-soil collectors, their respective liquids slopping over the sides of the buckets that dangled from their yokes, causing the street to brim with a dubious odour; come March or April, when the constant rains set in, clandestine new life forms began to flourish. Many of the inland immigrants, unused to the climate, found that the spaces in between their toes festered and became unbearably itchy, releasing an alarming stench whenever they took off their shoes.

Those refugees used to think often of how, one day, they would leave Valeria-administered Nevers and return home. But then the authoritarian Vanguard Party took over inland Ksana, establishing the Vanguard Republic and sealing off its borders. The refugees watched as one child was born, then another, each one leading to the next, all of them bouncing out to race around in the streets. Sometimes the refugees yelled at them, or chased them with feather dusters. Other times they simply watched them scamper away, these children who imitated foreigners, their mouths spewing a ghostly language their parents could barely understand. The refugees looked off to where there had once been bobbing ocean waves and wondered when all the water had turned to concrete. Valeria Island's coastline had vanished into the distance, extending the tiny land mass outwards. A train line ran across the newly claimed ground. Meanwhile the refugees felt as if they, and the city they had lived in for so much of their lives, had transformed from solid entities into slippery illusions.

The daytrippers contentedly strolling the Valeria Island streets with Professor Q were second-generation immigrants. They were ladies and gentlemen of the petite bourgeoisie, raised during the era of the city's breakneck development, used to everything being a competition—and, having emerged victorious from these competitions, they were now unapologetically smug about their achievements. In all their long years, most of them had never once ventured

9

over to socialist Ksana, although when their parents made the trip they gave them extra banknotes to make up for it, and had them deliver box after box of gifts to the relatives left behind in their ancestral hometowns. They felt no particular sense of national consciousness and didn't believe in linguistic purism. Among friends they usually spoke Southern, the language that had spread through the region, but they used the written form of Ksanese mixed with Southern slang for their personal correspondence and reverted to their respective hometown dialects for interactions with their parents. In their capacity as local elites, however, they composed official correspondence in Valerian, and sat around in public places ostentatiously reading Valerian-language newspapers rather than Ksanese ones.

And Professor Q? None of them knew anything about his past. He had appeared among them as Maria's husband: a short man with wavy hair always combed from an unsophisticated centre parting. From some angles his skin appeared so dark it was almost blue, like that of the labourers who arrived in Nevers from places further south, while in other lights he looked fair enough to pass as one of the Western colonizers. Even more bewildering was that not only did he speak fluent Southern and Valerian, he also knew languages the rest of them had never even heard of. If any of them enquired about his nationality or place of birth, he would only smile, or glance shyly at Maria and reply with the Ksanese proverb: *You marry a cat, you follow the cat. You marry a bird, you follow the bird.*

The city on Valeria Island extended from the flattened area around the shoreline up into the mountains beyond it. The street with the antiques market gave way to a twisting road, and the group climbed steadily higher. The island's precipitous terrain offered a panoramic view of the harbour and peninsula, making it easy to understand why the original colonizers had chosen it as their strategic regional base. Yet, ten years earlier, the declining Valerian Empire had handed Nevers over like a gift to the Vanguard Republic, which was at that moment captivating audiences on the global stage. Having little faith in the new regime, several of the daytrippers had opted to leave. Then, as the years went by, they had all come back. Some returned without their partners, and others with greyer, sparser hair, their faces marked as if butterflies had flown over and left behind permanent shadows. Now, when they got together for meals, they still laughed as uproariously as they always had, revealing yellowing, gap-toothed smiles, and they still ordered like show-off yuppies, although they ate less and less. During the final phase of these gatherings there was always a white layer of congealed fat over the remaining meat and vegetables, the carcass of the picked-over fish, the half-full bowl of cooled soup.

The group commented on how, in the few short years of their absence, Nevers had constructed even more enormous glass commercial buildings, and even more housing blocks, shinier and skinnier than ever before. The labyrinthine back alleys were crammed with inquisitive inland Ksanese dragging bulky leather suitcases—the very same inlanders they had once considered impoverished country bumpkins, who now arrived with rolls of banknotes bursting from their pockets. Professor Q informed his companions that a number of the surviving high-end hotels, constructed a few years back to attract European guests with their 'colonial flair', had started to recruit staff proficient in Northern, the standardized language of inland Ksana. They were welcoming the inland nouveau riche to the penthouse suites. Up there, one press of a remote and the curtains would part to display the concrete flesh of the city, still frantically growing.

What the group had not noticed was that the majority of inland visitors were delivered en masse by tour buses to newly developed districts of Nevers, where they were stuffed like foam packing peanuts into hastily constructed, grandiose hotels that looked like bizarre space stations. These hotels were temporary stage sets thrown together for the benefit of tourists, with imitation marble floors and glittering false ceilings that would deteriorate within a couple of years, and cheap paintwork that rapidly stained and peeled. Every so often there would be a report hidden in the corner of the newspaper about a carelessly installed lift in free fall, the handful of tourists inside it vanishing forever into a dark hole underground. While the cross-border bridge from western Nevers to another Ksanese peninsula was under construction, a few workers lost their footing and fell into the sea—but those deaths were soundless deaths, unlike those of the new inland immigrants who jumped, one, then another, from the tops of buildings, landing with horrifying thuds, obliging cleaners to rush out and work overtime to scrub blood and brain matter from the pavements.

As the area first exploited by the colonizers, set up as their great international trading hub, Valeria Island was still home to most of the blue-eyed, golden-haired, fresh-faced foreigners in Nevers. All the finest, most long-standing restaurants were there, and so too was a distinctive, age-old atmosphere of arrogance, luxury, and indolence. Towards the end of their stroll, the group passed a stretch of luxury villas built into the seized mid-mountain territory, aggressively fortified with black iron gates. As they proceeded back down into the city centre, they heard fluttery strains of jazz music and found both sides of the alley taken up by swaying, half-drunk foreigners. Joking and whispering to one another in Southern, the group brushed past the foreigners as if they themselves were nothing but a band of happy tourists, with no connection whatsoever to the city. Professor Q was the only one who seemed mysteriously perturbed. His ears were humming like organ pipes, and the red lips of the foreigner women rose to dance before his eyes, while their breasts undulated in the dim evening light.

The group continued until they reached a little snake restaurant, where they settled themselves around an octagonal wooden table to dine on duck liver sausages and a congee-like snake soup scattered with chrysanthemum petals. Grease soon coated the insides of their mouths, and their peals of laughter ricocheted off the walls like disturbed pigeons. Meanwhile, Professor Q felt everything around him turn black, and his mouth go painfully dry.

The following day Professor Q stayed in bed with a high fever, his throat so hoarse he had to ask Maria to call in sick to the university on his behalf. That evening, barely conscious, he was taken to a nearby clinic, where the poisonous scent of disinfectant assaulted his nostrils, and young, flutter-eyed nurses took turns giggling behind a glass screen. The waiting room was so cold that even the sofas seemed to have turned blue with it.

In an examination room, a doctor instructed him to undress and lie back in a leather chair. The professor felt his body become passive and feminine, an object for the doctor's obscene icy stethoscope to probe wherever it liked, touching on intimate, wrinkled folds of skin. He glanced at the doctor in alarm, then his vision cleared and he realized that this was David! David, who had returned many years ago from his medical studies in Valeria as a prematurely ageing young man, his hair already half gone. Keeping to the usual routine, David pressed the professor's fat, reddened tongue with a popsicle stick and shone a tiny light onto his white-speckled uvula.

'Your throat is a little inflamed,' he said.

Every autumn since Professor Q had settled in Nevers, he now recalled, the air had carried in it a toxin he did not seem able to adapt to, causing him to bring his inflamed throat to David's clinic. He no longer felt afraid; after all, the doctor's implements could only probe the most superficial parts of his reality.

As he had done all the other times before, David prescribed

Professor Q two bottles of a red medicine to be taken morning, noon, and night. Back at home, Maria insisted that the professor eat porridge with honey before taking his first dose. She pressed a hand to his forehead like a clergywoman bestowing her blessings, and whispered: 'Perhaps it was the snake. Or maybe just a bad wind off the sea.'

Two days later, his fever abated, Professor Q returned to Lone Boat University, in the Green Moss district of the Nevers peninsula, and went to sit in his custom-made ergonomic office chair. Bach's 'Air on the G String' emanated from two high-quality speakers on his desk. He liked to listen to classical music while doing his grading; this way, he was less likely to spend the time muttering derisively about his students being a bunch of illiterates, before descending into self-recriminations over how he had ended up reduced to this, a hack teacher in a debased, cultureless little city. He had been working all morning when he finally abandoned his computer mouse and inter-laced his fingers over the little paunch of his belly. Once again, he found his gaze travelling to the painting hanging on the wall opposite.

It was inside a gilt frame he had commissioned for it not too long before, and depicted an upright, shadowy figure, who seemed to be a man wearing a suit. Beside him was a voluptuous nude ballet dancer, arms crossed, standing en pointe. Professor Q had not been able to establish the gender of the ballet dancer, because although he or she had a pair of full, rounded breasts, the rest of the body was hard and muscular, and a long, fleshy rod stood up from between the legs, one end pressing against the soft outline of the shadow— whether readying to launch an attack or in the process of copulation, it was impossible to say.

All four walls of the professor's office were painted an indifferent white. Behind him, two steel bookshelves were neatly lined with Valerian dictionaries, twenty years' worth of short-story annuals from the same publishing house, and a few literary criticism primers. He kept the room free of personal snapshots or leafy plants, cultivating a serious, ascetic mood for his workplace. Clearly, the painting wasn't at all in keeping with this aim.

It had been sent to his office in a large envelope bearing the Lone Boat University insignia. The envelope had no name or return address on it and he hadn't recognized the handwriting, although he had felt a strange sensation of having seen the painting somewhere before. Something about it must have been familiar, he reasoned, for him to have kept it, because that decision certainly had nothing to do with the artist's technique or subject matter.

Now, back in his office after his illness, he once again considered the painting. He decided the two figures were definitely not still, but rather in the middle of some kind of repetitive motion, trying to convey a message to him. Their rhythm sucked him in, and, although it was barely perceptible, he felt sure his office was swaying; he turned off the music coming from his speakers and the room shook as though weightless. He gripped his chair and took a deep breath. A few sounds lingered, very faintly, somewhere in the distance.

Turning towards the window, he didn't immediately see the world that lay outside. Instead, he was confronted by the expressionless slats of his window blinds—white, clean, office-appropriate. He tended to keep them pulled down, to avoid other people's gazes intruding on his private domain. He walked over and pushed through two fingers, pressing down to create a narrow crack through which he saw sunlight glinting off leaves and, further back, the omnipresent mountains. He also saw the eyes.

Even before going over to the window, he had known this symptom persisted. He was still seeing her eyes, their colour shifting like that of a flowing river. The day of the Valeria antiques market she'd been in a display window, these eyes of hers staring out at him through the glass.

He'd thought it odd that only he seemed to notice. How could the others have missed her? She was stark naked and glaringly pale, hugging her knees to her chest, her body curled into a ball. Her translucent, waxy skin made her luminous. She had been sitting there in the window, apparently just another forgotten old curio among crystal chandeliers, old-fashioned wall clocks, colourful cut-glass goblets, strands of plastic pearls, and piles of scratched glasses frames. Her body was perfectly still, but her face peered up from between her legs, her eyes fixed intently on the professor.

He tried not to look, but she persisted in his field of vision. Like a stereoscopic illusion, she seemed lifelike, and right in front of him, even when there was no way it was really her that he was seeing. Was the hair coiled so elegantly on the back of her head golden brown or chestnut? Her skin was so pale, almost corpse-like, but her vision seemed all-encompassing, as if she had a 360-degree view of the world.

Professor Q retracted his fingers from the blinds and closed his eyes. He decided to go for a little walk, to get his body moving after the previous two days of rest.

3

Lone Boat University had been built on a hillside. The surrounding area was developed relatively late, meaning that although recent years had seen a spate of new construction projects, it was still possible to climb the road to the university, look out across Cloudy Harbour and the mountains around it, and imagine oneself in a bucolic scene from an ancient Ksanese poem. Professor Q's grey office building was halfway up the hill. If you carried on a little way past it, you reached a grassy slope, at the top of which was an old copper bell, once struck every midday but now left idle. It had been a gift from the colonial administration to mark the founding of the university, intended as a token of their support for this seat of classical Ksanese learning. The demure elderly man beside the bell, also cast in copper, was the founding father; one of the great Confucian scholars who had fled south to Nevers several decades earlier. He was bowing slightly, and held his fingertips pressed together into an arch, making him look almost deferential. Deferential, except that his right eyebrow and the right corner of his mouth twitched upwards, as though barely suppressing a smirk. From time to time, Professor Q would wonder who the Confucian's derision was aimed at. Himself? The people of Nevers? He had been persecuted by the Vanguard regime and come to Nevers seeking asylum, but had it really been his life's goal to cultivate his immense talents in such an infernally hot, humid, colonized, barbarous little place? His eyes were squinting and unfocused, and there was something unsettling about his expression—he had the face of a vaudeville performer who might, at any moment, reach into his pockets and produce an assortment of juggling balls.

On this particular day, Professor Q decided not to head up to the bell and statue, but instead to stroll downhill. The autumn term was drawing to a close, and fewer and fewer students were coming in for class. He could almost hear the hillside sighing with relief. Nearby, the copper spouts of the library fountain stubbornly continued to spit mouthfuls of white foam into the air at abrupt, regular intervals. As he drew level with the fountain, he noticed two colleagues from the Valerian literature department walking straight towards him.

They usually looked so gloomy, with never a good word to say about anyone. What were they doing now acting all cheery, waving enthusiastically in his direction? Professor Q kept his head down and veered away, pretending not to have seen, ducking behind a row of evergreen bushes he didn't know the name for and turning onto a different path.

He had been at Lone Boat for over a decade but had always kept his interactions with other academics to a minimum. In his expensive, old-fashioned suits, his face fixed in an expression of unwavering calm, he showed up punctually to each faculty and academic meeting. During these meetings he declined to comment on the vast majority of topics, in fact refused to talk at all unless it was absolutely necessary, and vanished the moment they were over. He considered this perfectly acceptable behaviour because, in his heart of hearts, he felt it was not really him participating in the meetings, but rather a suit-wearing, tie-sporting, flesh-and-blood mannequin version of himself.

He felt sorry for this poor mannequin who had to sit at a desk day in, day out, composing research proposals, applying for research funding he had no need for whatsoever. He was like a cement worker, dumping dry, insipid words into research-paper-shaped moulds, turning out cautious essays in which he scrambled to turn a few popular opinions into shadow versions of themselves or else hid behind theories, finding new ways to perform other people's voices in order to win the approval of his peers. Then there were the endless forms, each one a little different than the last, all of them requiring him to boast wildly about his output to prove the continued value of his existence.

He had repeatedly studied the department's employee handbook (because the requirements kept changing). So far as he could tell, not a single one of his performance evaluation forms had failed to meet the department's targets and yet, while most teaching staff who joined at the same time as him had been promoted, he remained a lowly assistant professor. On top of this, every two years he was required to compile yet another thick stack of reports, and then to wait in terror while the powers that be deliberated over whether or not to renew his contract.

At the last review meeting, the faculty dean had smiled almost cordially, then picked up Professor Q's file and rapidly read aloud his performance rating for each listed item. He concluded by declaring his overall assessment: 'Excellent!' Then added: 'Unfortunately, your promotion has not been approved.'

The performance evaluation file was confidential. As the professor was not permitted to see it, he had paid close attention to every word that left the dean's mouth during the meeting, afraid one small lapse could mean missing something crucial. But the dean spoke so rapidly, and he was such a busy person . . . From his seat in one corner of the dean's cavernous office, Professor Q could see mountainous stacks of files arranged precariously on the dean's desk, and smell decomposing meat wafting from fast-food packaging in the wastepaper bin beneath. He blamed the malignant odour for his flagging concentration; he wished the dean would slow down a little, but he didn't have the courage to interrupt him. Then, just as the dean finally lifted his eyes from the report, the professor heard himself exclaim: 'Sir—'

The face across from him stiffened, its surface pulling so taut it seemed in danger of splitting open. He steeled himself and pressed on: 'Seeing . . . seeing as there are no issues with my performance, may I ask why . . . why my application has been unsuccessful?'

For a few seconds the dean remained motionless, like a coin-operated automaton whose money had run out. Professor Q's back was sweating. He was aware of the secretary glaring at him from over by the door, her smile extending only as far as her cheeks, but he refused to give up: this was his chance.

'If . . . if there's anything else I can do—'

The dean waved at him to be quiet and, with a weary laugh, reopened the file and began to leaf through, as if seeing it properly for the very first time.

'Well, let's see. Awarded two research grants, attended four international conferences this year, published three papers, all in top-tier journals . . . why has your application been unsuccessful? You have to understand, the university operates according to an established procedure. There are an enormous number of levels involved, and this isn't down to any individual decision-maker—'

The dean was talking less rapidly now, but so quietly that the professor had to draw closer to hear what he was saying. As he leaned in, he couldn't resist glancing back at the secretary. She had opened the door, as though to show him the two suit-clad professors outside, sitting bolt upright on the sofa. Both were staring at him, clearly furious at his extended occupancy of the dean's office. But what was the dean saying? By the time Professor Q had turned back to face him, his lips were sealed. The two of them were so close that the professor could see the hair peeping out from the other man's nostrils. He sprang to his feet, sending his chair clattering to the ground.

Professor Q couldn't remember the details of his frenzied escape from the dean's office, but the negative effect of his brazen enquiries quickly became apparent. For several nights in a row he found himself unable to fall asleep, despite Maria's nightly administration of a soothing cup of tea. Sometimes, he regretted being so impulsive and making such a bad impression on not only the dean, but also on that secretary of his, which would no doubt have a direct impact on his next application for renewal. Other times, he chastised himself for not taking things further, for not seizing the chance to ask: 'If my performance is so excellent, then is there something I'm doing wrong while filling in the form or writing my self-evaluation—perhaps some wording or formatting issue I've overlooked?'

He'd heard there was a knack to padding out the forms and reports, a few magical code words known only to those senior members of university staff who carried out the appraisals; secrets rarely revealed to lowly assistant professors.

But some people always found a way. They always found a way to get more insider information than he could.

More recently, a rare knock had sounded at his office door. Dressed in a pair of skinny jeans and a shirt that had been ironed to smooth perfection, his teeth brilliant white, his hair black and lustrous, the newly hired Professor W had cracked open the door and bashfully requested a word of advice. Rather than feeling irritated by the intrusion, Professor Q had found it amusing. He hadn't joined the university until he was well into middle age, and his hair was by now completely grey—could it be that W had not yet realized he was one of the department's lowest-ranking professors? That he had not yet been awarded tenure, meaning the university could terminate his employment at any time?

The mannequin version of Professor Q did not turn W away. On the contrary, he allowed him to come inside, open up a folding chair, solemnly sit down, and then launch into an enthusiastic account of his research projects and upcoming conferences. Professor Q kept his head down and nodded from time to time, doing his best not to let on to the young man that he wasn't actually listening. Instead, he was inspecting his shadow, examining its dusky blue colour and tracing its loose, wavering outline with his eyes.

But if the Professor Q sitting there hunched over in his seat was just a mannequin, then where, he wondered, had the real him gone?

That day on the Lone Boat University campus, as he turned down the path behind the bushes, Professor Q was delighted to have broken free from his colleagues. The path led to the university canteen and was a popular spot for student organizations to set up makeshift fundraising stands, selling books and handicrafts to passers-by. He'd assumed there wouldn't be any students around so late in the term, but a cluster of girls lingered up ahead, holding what looked like stacks of yellow flyers. Judging by their risqué outfits, they weren't there to evangelize; most likely they were promoting some sort of dance event, or else were from one of the new political organizations. Student political movements had been increasingly active since the Vanguard Republic had assumed control of Nevers. Several years previously, a Lone Boat student had scaled a colonial-era Valerian clock tower and hugged the enormous hands as they pointed to twelve o'clock, preventing it from being demolished. Another time, students involved with the farmland protection movement had dressed up in white monk robes and laid themselves down in the road, until finally the police came and carried them off by their hands and feet, the bodies swaying as they went. Yet another time, apparently in protest at a modification to high school history textbooks, students had arrived made up like actors from a gruesome play to an exam he was invigilating, with fake knives stuck through their heads and blood running down their faces.

From the way these girls were dressed and made-up, he couldn't tell exactly what activity they were promoting. Once he was a little closer, he could see that their skin-tight t-shirts were emblazoned with a distorted version of the character for 'move'. Presumably some kind of logo? New student political organizations were constantly being set up and shut down; it was impossible to keep track of all their names and causes.

Professor Q neither wanted to return to his previous path nor to be mobbed by the students. He planned to keep his head down and briskly pass them by, but no sooner had he formulated this plan than one of the girls started waving. From a distance, he'd been convinced he didn't know any of them, but now he could see the eyes again. He started to tremble, feeling that the scene was shifting. He froze. As the waving girl made a beeline for him, he noticed someone nod at her approvingly, their gaze studiously avoiding her wind-ruffled skirt hem and the undulating outline of her chest. Someone else came to walk beside her, their tongue slick and ghoulish, their eyes glowing. The stack of yellow flyers the girl had been handing out like lucky charms slipped from her fingers and floated to the ground. In almost the same moment, Professor Q sped up, racing past her and through the university gates, where he leapt into a taxi.

He hadn't considered where he was going, and was pleased to hear his mouth make the decision for him: 'To Valeria Island!'

4

Professor Q lived in a residential complex in Lion Slope, still on the Nevers peninsula but quite some distance from the university. Like the majority of areas developed during the city's economic boom, pragmatism had been the guiding principle for the neighbourhood's design: the tower blocks were orderly and narrow, every inch meticulously calculated to ensure that each part served a purpose, leaving no ambiguous blank space to spark unnecessary flights of imagination. Maria had chosen their flat and made the down payment on it, and the flat itself was objectively dull and uninspiring. Even so, the first time the professor had seen the title deeds, with his name written in beside his wife's, he had been unspeakably moved.

He turned one of the two bedrooms into a study, a kind of private collecting room exclusively for him. Every week without fail he would go to the bookshop to buy new books, and every year on his trips to international conferences and on his holidays abroad he seized the chance to go shopping, gathering exotic paintings, statues, photograph albums, and rare books, all of which he would pack into the room on his return.

He had so many books that it was impossible to stick to any kind of system for looking after them properly. Before long, new purchases were covered in dust and the humidity would swoop in to attack, leaving them soft and spotted with mildew. Perhaps he did it on purpose, willing them to turn dark and disorderly, because when the pages warped into messy waves, or gaped open like perpetually parted lips, they formed beautiful little hidey-holes for booklice, cockroaches, and all sorts of other tiny dark things. In this way, he accumulated nooks and crannies that Maria would never notice, in which he could bury all those treasures she would almost certainly have dismissed as creepy, or depraved.

If you were to enter the chaos and forge ahead to the bookcases that lined the walls, you would notice that they were tall but also deep, each shelf crammed with double rows of books. And if you pulled over a ladder and climbed up to reach for the highest shelf— well, you'd be able to imagine Professor Q doing the same thing himself. Up there, having removed the first layer of books, he would discover poems he had published as a young man, impassioned screeds he would now characterize as 'hormone-addled'. Alongside, tucked away in a few old notebooks, were clippings of columns he had written and interviews he had once given. He would stand at the top of the ladder and observe these relics without ever reaching for them, as if they were domino tiles—one touch and the whole world would come tumbling down. Instead, with the precision of a master bricklayer, he would replace the front row of books, rebuilding the outer wall and thereby accomplishing the task of forgetting everything behind it all over again.

Maria could have been standing at the door to the study at exactly that moment and still she would have felt no desire to enter. She was not interested in poking through her husband's books or inspecting his collected diversions. In her opinion, he was a hoarder, plain and simple. He made sow's ears of silk purses, bringing all those shiny, expensive objects into his squalid world only for them to decay and be forgotten. She had made a single, futile attempt to set the study to rights. Since then, she had given up, resorting to squirting in jasmine perfume every so often, like a priest sprinkling holy water to drive out demons.

Very few friends were invited into Professor Q's home. During his everyday comings and goings he would slam the front door closed if he so much as caught sight of the little boy from the flat opposite. But, occasionally, the boy would manage to glimpse the enormous woodblock print of Mephistopheles hanging on the wall outside the study, or the copper wire sculpture of Don Quixote holding a tiny spear on the living room coffee table. At first these unfamiliar foreign faces had been frightening, but the more often he saw them the more ridiculous they seemed. The same was true of Professor Q, drifting along the hallway in his old-fashioned suits, that other-worldly look in his eyes. He seemed unaware of how his comfortable life had come to manifest itself in his body, for example in the excess flesh dangling from his neck, flapping from side to side as he walked.

Professor Q and his wife regularly accompanied each other downstairs to stretch their legs and cast an appreciative eye over the neighbourhood's neatly pruned hedges. They would pause together in front of the tiny pond to watch the koi carp swimming around in circles, each on its own invisible orbit. Occasionally they would spy an enormous freshwater turtle, sometimes just its head creeping out from among the slippery rocks, and other times the whole creature, still as a fossil. In this little neighbourhood of theirs, with its impeccably clean streets, swept punctually at the same time every day, it was rare for anything unexpected to occur. Or, at least, for signs of the unexpected to linger for very long.

Maria and Professor Q strolled shoulder to shoulder in a rhythm established and honed over the course of many years: they rounded the corner, walked to the end of the street, turned around, came back again. Unless they happened to run into a neighbour, when of course this rhythm was disrupted. Maria would smile warmly then, while the professor pursed his lips; he would involuntarily recoil and find his shoulders shifting forward to compensate, his neck craning like a turtle's. Maria's footsteps would pause as she and the neighbour exchanged pleasantries, although heaven knows what exactly was being said—Professor Q may have been standing at Maria's side, his expression mild, maintaining a veneer of politeness, but in his imagination he was still walking, headed down a fork in the path that Maria didn't even know existed. In these moments his brows relaxed and his dangling flesh ceased to flap about and, his soul thus freed from his physical form, he felt secretly pleased with himself.

Here or not here, he thought, it's all a state of mind!

He would never have admitted it to anyone, but he was immensely grateful his wife's job kept her trapped inside a government office building a minimum of five days a week. It meant that when he left his own office before sundown he didn't need to come up with excuses for staying out late; he could simply take himself across the harbour and wander around Valeria Island to his heart's content. He loved to amble the island's narrow alleyways, revelling in their colonial charm and browsing the bookshops before heading to a bar and settling into a seat by the window. There was nothing untoward about it; he didn't go to bars to flirt with barmaids. Instead, he would sip a gin or a whisky while looking out at the street, where white people walked past in groups of two or three, all of them dressed in majestic overcoats and impossibly shiny shoes. Sometimes he would spot one of the female domestic workers that the Nevers government encouraged its citizens to hire cheaply from countries further south, her dark skin threaded with blue and her hands busy with someone else's children, or someone else's dog. Often, like a stab of sudden sunshine, she would flash him a smile. He always smiled back, although what he was really watching was not the scenery, or the passers-by, but his own reflection in the glass. The glass had a mystical quality: it made his eyes blur and his skin colour hard to determine. In his reflection, he was a free man, a bachelor, a foreigner sojourning alone in the city, idly debating where to head to next. Behind him, someone threw down dice, setting each individual die spinning in unison; when they settled, their numbers would be revealed, like answers from an oracle. But for now those answers were a secret, the dice hidden beneath a black cup.

The day Professor Q dashed off the Lone Boat campus into a passing taxi, he had no intention of browsing bookshops or sitting around in bars. He had to find the owner of the eyes, and so he went back to the street with the antiques market. Now that he was there alone, the dinginess of the goods came into clearer focus. Only a few other shoppers were out, all of them intently picking through displays in search of treasure. They crouched down and found themselves in thrall to the peculiar magic of the bric-a-brac, which compelled them to fill their plastic trays with miniature figurines of Jesus, Shiva, and fat-bellied laughing Buddhas.

At every intersection Professor Q expected to see the two-storey shophouse from the day of his birthday outing. He recalled that it had still had its original structure, the first floor jutting out over the street to create a shady arcade supported by pillars. The shopfront, in contrast, was a modern glass display case, with *her* and the other old goods fixed in place behind the window.

As he continued down the street, he found himself increasingly unable to see the objects laid out in front of him. The road had transformed into a pedestrian thoroughfare. He had no idea where all these people had come from; they seemed to have burst out from sewers and behind doors, surging around him like floodwater. The current carried him along until those at the front slowed to a halt, causing the crowd to pool into a circle. He wasn't a tall man and found himself pressed behind two white men, obliged to peer up through their armpits to glimpse what was happening at the centre.

Standing in the middle of the crowd was a mime, his face painted white, his hands splayed against an imaginary wall. He was trapped in a tiny room, in which he sat on air to eat his dinner, then sat on air to go to the toilet (holding his nose against the stench), then curled into a ball for a nap.

Professor Q's gaze travelled past the mime to see that the shop-house lay just beyond, although he couldn't see its pillars, nor the glass display case, because both had been screened off by an enormous noticeboard. The area immediately in front of the board thronged with exuberant onlookers.

The mime ate again, defecated again, went back to sleep. Food appeared at regular intervals, delivered into the room through a hidden trapdoor. The mime tried to peer through the trapdoor, to no avail. He dejectedly ate the food he had been given, then went to the toilet, then curled up to sleep. The room must have smelled atrocious by this stage, but he continued with the cycle: eat, shit, sleep. Professor Q marvelled at how the audience remained so captivated, and in such high spirits. They sipped contentedly on juice and fizzy drinks, and chewed little pellets of gum, while the mime banged desperately on walls and then went back, yet again, to sitting on air.

Sometime later, another mime appeared, his face also painted white. He paid no attention to the man trapped inside the room. Instead, clutching a stack of cards, he marched up to the audience, only for the audience to disperse, vanishing so quickly that, within seconds, only a handful of spectators remained.

The professor was delighted. Finally, he could see the noticeboard properly! It depicted a swanlike ballerina in a white tutu, bending forward with her arms opened wide, her eyes aimed directly at him. Standing behind her, wearing a cloak, top hat, and opera mask, was a magician. Professor Q began to shake. There was no doubt about it: he recognized this pale-faced young woman. At that moment, the second mime appeared in front of him, plucked a card from his stack, and, as though passing a secret note, pressed it meaningfully into his palm. From the card, the professor learned that the young woman—Aliss, the Music-Box Ballerina—would be performing next month, in this same location, in a show hosted by the magician.

When he looked up from the card, the performers had vanished, just like the crowd. Cards were scattered all over the ground. Everyone else in the street seemed to have somewhere they needed to be, the mime show already forgotten. Professor Q was the only one hurrying over to the noticeboard, which had been fastened to two pillars at the corner of the street. Between the pillars and the board's wooden frame was a small gap. He pushed his head through it and discovered that the items in the window display had changed. There was new glassware, some embroidery, and, as a centrepiece, with beady black eyes and a Santa hat on its head, a giant bear. From the reflection in the creature's eyes, Professor Q had a clear view of his own pathetic roly-poly torso and aged head, tragically stuck between the board and pillar, afraid to exert any force in either direction, for fear of tearing the whole thing down.

5

In truth, we already know Professor Q's fate: he is going to fall in love with the beautiful doll named Aliss. He might have been a little slow on the uptake, reluctant to admit it even to himself, but the signs had been there all along, since well before he turned fifty and officially embarked on the affair.

A few months before his birthday, in accordance with his own past instructions, he received a parcel. It arrived one morning soon after Maria had left their flat, setting off for work in the government administration building.

Five days out of seven, Maria was through the door before seven thirty, wearing no make-up and sporting either a white shirt and trouser suit or what looked like a grey nurse's smock. From a young age, she had made very clear demands of her clothes and cosmetics: not to attract attention. This was partly attributable to her convent education, but was mostly a limitation she imposed upon herself. When girls at school had rebelled by making modifications to their uniforms, sometimes covertly, other times bold as day, their behaviour had mystified Maria. The way she saw it, the less she stood out, the better.

She was always on the train platform by seven forty-five, and the train would arrive within two minutes, occasionally three. The service seldom ran any later than that—in fact it was renowned for its punctuality—but it was no match for the precise workings of Maria's internal clock. She was a natural leader, had been ever since her school days; as one of the nuns had once commented, her iron self-discipline had the effect of pulling everyone around her into line. And indeed, the moment she stepped outside the flat that morning, the meticulous order she had imposed within it began to unravel.

Feeling free and relaxed in the quiet of his empty home, Professor Q sipped coffee with a dash of whisky and browsed a collection of classic Valerian-language satirical essays. He settled on one by the seventeenth-century author Joss Pigin. Little is known about Pigin; it is entirely possible that the name is a pseudonym. Pigin's prose is sophisticated and assured but also bitingly funny, and the professor was thoroughly enjoying himself, chuckling appreciatively as he read, until he was interrupted by the unexpected ring of the doorbell. At first it sounded less like a doorbell and more like the plaintive wail of an animal, but the wail soon morphed into the doorbell's distinctive, apocalyptic tune, prodding the professor out of his reverie. He stood up and went to press himself against the front door, peering suspiciously through the spyhole. There he saw the familiar face of the neighbourhood postman.

The postman handed over a lightweight package, smirking suggestively. Then he winked. Professor Q forced a stiff little smile in response.

Once he had made sure the door was firmly closed, obliterating the postman's face, he felt calmer again and began wondering what the package might be. It was too light for a book, surely? The handwriting on the label was elegant but didn't call to mind anyone he knew. According to the stamps, it had come from Eiffely. He couldn't think of any friends there, or any connection he might have to a local college or university. He opened it carefully. Inside was a thirty-inch doll, tightly bundled in transparent bubble wrap. Her eyes were closed as though fast asleep and she seemed to be breathing, but shallowly, as if on the verge of suffocation. He tore off the wrapping and her thick eyelashes blinked open, bringing to a life a pair of brilliant blue eyes.

The doll wore a short pink tutu and a silver bodice decorated with two shell-like cups. Her pouting lips seemed to simper at the professor, as though to say, *I'm a good girl*—with mischievous implications. Her expression jogged his memory: they had met in that town in Eiffely, outside the door to a little shop. She had been behind the window glass, smiling at him just like this.

That had been six months or so earlier, when he and Maria were in Eiffely on a trip. Tour group activities had finished for the day, and the two of them had broken away from the other travellers and gone to sit in a nearby open-air café. Professor Q ordered a gin and Maria an orange juice with mint. Maria considered reminding her husband that it was only three in the afternoon, a little early for alcohol, but the people around them seemed to have been drinking since the moment they woke up, and she held her tongue.

In the plaza around the café, a band of musicians fiddled with their instruments, playing in a casual, fragmented way that could have been tuning up but then again could have been the start of a performance. Maria didn't care much about music and started chatting to a small boy at the next table, using a combination of exaggerated facial expressions, hand gestures, and a few simple words of Eiffelian.

The boy made Professor Q uncomfortable. His eyes were open abnormally wide, but that wasn't it; it was his deadened stare, and the way all his movements seemed stiff and in slow motion.

This kid is hopeless, thought the professor, although he knew better than to share the thought with Maria.

He tried to focus on the music, briefly even quite enjoying it, but then his attention wandered. He glanced at his wife and saw that she was holding the boy's hand. Then he noticed his glass was empty.

'I'm going for a walk,' he announced.

Maria nodded without really listening, distracted by the boy's mother, who was in the process of unfurling a ribbon, apparently trying to explain something. When Maria eventually turned, hoping her husband would come to her aid with his more fluent Eiffelian, she discovered that he had left her behind, and that each narrow alleyway leading off the plaza looked exactly the same. The place was a maze. Then she caught sight of him walking into the distance, plump and ungainly but shrinking to nothing before her eyes. She wanted to call out, but it was too late.

One of the alleyways drifted towards the professor, and one display window led to another, then another. Displays of identical glass earrings and necklaces led to displays of scarves, which looked surprisingly high quality—pure silk, with elegant orchid patterns. He considered buying one for Maria, imagining how he would put it in a box and gently nudge it to her across the dinner table. But it would only lead to days of nagging. She would complain about him wasting money, and he would end up back in the shop asking for a refund, or to exchange the scarf for something practical, like a thermos. He carried on down the alley until he came to a window display of cloth lampshades and hand-cranked cameras. He paused, finding that the glare on the window prevented him from seeing in clearly, and then felt himself drawn closer. That was how he had first caught sight of her.

She was doing the forward splits, with her arms curved out and up, as though readying for a dolphin to leap through. Her head was angled haughtily away so that he could see only the back, with its towering bun, and the long, elegant line of her neck. He shuffled along until he could see her face, which was when he discovered her mouth, with its sly, schoolgirl smile.

He smiled back, involuntarily raising his hand. A hunched old man emerged from the shop.

'What beauty!' exclaimed Professor Q, in stilted Eiffelian.

The old man clasped his hands behind his back.

'No such thing as beautiful or unbeautiful here,' he said. 'You see what you want to see.'

Professor Q entered the shop, where he found ram and ox heads mounted on the wall, and a carriage clock with a face that suddenly split open, dividing into pieces like flower petals to reveal the spinning mechanisms behind. He rifled idly through a basket of old postcards and pin buttons, before walking outside again to take another look at the doll.

The old man stayed inside and began dusting the glass counter around the till.

'In case you're interested,' he said, raising his voice a little, 'she's a Dolligal.'

The professor turned.

'I can't take her right now,' he replied.

The old man glanced at him but made no further comment.

Professor Q went back inside and pulled a wad of cash from his pocket, then groped around for his fountain pen. He picked up a name card lying on the counter, flipped it over, and scrawled a few lines on the back.

'My address. You can post her.'

By the time Professor Q made it back to the café, Maria's orange juice was all gone and the musicians were on a break, sitting on some railings around a flowerbed. Maria was beaming, and showed her husband a rope knot the boy had made for her. It was a traditional Ksanese handicraft, and she had just taught him how to do it. She was met with one of the professor's rare, warm smiles, which she took to mean that perhaps he didn't dislike children as much as he always claimed. In reality, he hadn't noticed his wife's hard-won trophy—he was staring off to some vague point beyond her, thinking of the Dolligal's outstretched thighs. He looked down and watched his shadow contract beneath the sun, trying his hardest to contain his excitement.

Of course, Professor Q had other dolls. The flaxen-haired princess, for starters, stumbled upon while wandering in a seaside bazaar. She had a delicate neck, a cool, indifferent expression on her upwards-tilted face, and long golden locks tied back with a bow. But the body beneath her neck was missing, and when he found her she'd looked like a guillotined princess, her head stranded amid filthy porcelain tableware and stacks of vinyl records. He felt desperately sorry for her, especially considering her vendor, some ignorant junk collector without the faintest idea of her plight. Even so, it had not occurred to him to buy her. At least, not until she called out: *Dear, kind professor, only you can save me! Please, rescue me from this chaos!*

He squatted down and peered into her glass eyes. There was nothing pitiful about her gaze. She looked like one of those high-quality toys produced in Limbody in the eighteenth century, modelled after a European girl of about fourteen. She was made of unglazed porcelain, giving her a rosy pink colour and flesh-like grain. As he looked her over, Professor Q felt goose pimples rise on his body.

The second doll was completely different. He called this one Papaya Girl. She came in a tattered cotton outfit, like something a beggar would wear. There were no discernible contours to her face, which may have been by design but could equally have been just the wear and tear of passing years. Her arms and legs were disproportionately long and she had slim little fingers that kept a tight grip on the hem of her top. She was fitted with a special internal mechanism: one twist of the key in the base beneath her feet and she would flutter her eyes and raise her arms, flashing a pair of drooping, papaya-shaped breasts.

The third doll was more crudely fashioned. She was a tiny Black girl in a dress that billowed in the style of Marilyn Monroe's, her hands reaching to press it down. If he hadn't picked her up, hankering after a glimpse of the delights that lay beneath that windswept skirt, he would never have realized she was a sauce bottle: if you poked your fingers up underneath her clothes, you reached a removable rubber stopper. Her body was porcelain but her head was made of soft, squeezable rubber; Professor Q would pinch and the sauce he'd loaded in, the ketchup or mustard or pesto . . . well, he could hold her up and watch those different colours gush from inside her, catching them on his finger. He would suck on the finger like a little boy, imagining he was tasting the juices of a real woman.

Maria had never seen this collection. The dolls were carefully locked away in a cupboard in Professor Q's study. The cupboard didn't look particularly large and was painted so that it blended easily into its surroundings. That's to say, it was painted a forgettable colour and, perhaps because of this, Professor Q himself often forgot it existed. But as soon as he opened its door, he would marvel all over again at how deep and wide it was, and how compelling its contents. Some things are like that: their presence feels indelible until you push them out of sight and they disappear, at least for a while.

When the Dolligal finally arrived from the not-so-distant past, Professor Q couldn't resist bringing his chubby fingers to the back of her dress to undo its dainty metallic buttons. He pulled the lacy tutu down over her long, slender legs and swabbed her with a baby wipe, cleaning away accumulated dust to reveal the lovely pink of her PVC skin. His fingers roamed her body. It was voluptuous, the body of an adult woman, but her breasts and pubic area were perfectly smooth. He plunged his hands into a plastic basin of glinting soapy bubbles and gently rinsed her tiny ballerina outfit, then dried it with his hairdryer. In the meantime, he had no choice but to leave her naked on his desk, where she jumped and slid and pirouetted on top of a pile of philosophy books.

Professor Q was blissfully happy all afternoon, right up until he went to put the Dolligal in his cupboard and saw the other dolls, long since stowed away, at which point he felt compelled to take them out for a wash, too. Yes, all Professor Q intended to do was to give those dolls a bath. He didn't exactly plan to try out the princess's head on different bodies (a wooden horse? a spider? the Holy Bible?) or to make Papaya Girl flip up her top and put on a show, although that was what he did. Later, in a flash of inspiration, he decided that to celebrate the new addition he would unscrew Marilyn's head, pour in a shot of whisky, and let the golden liquid trickle straight from her body into his mouth. What a treat for his tongue! It probed that secret territory, not stopping even when the friction from the unglazed surface started to grate; not even when his tongue started to bleed.

By the time Maria returned home from work (late at night, as always) everything was back in its place and the house was just as she had left it. She took off her coat and went into the bedroom, where she turned on a reading lamp and found Professor Q fast asleep. She gently stroked his forehead. It looked engorged, like a vessel full of dreams, and his mouth was tightly closed, as though guarding secrets. Secrets including his lacerated tongue, and the sweet memories that still flowed from it. Maria leaned in, close enough that she could smell the blood, but she mistook its source: noticing that the window was ajar, she assumed the smell was from the sea, carried in on the black night-time breeze. After all, sea breezes often do come mixed with blood—or, at least, they smell as if they do. Maria went over and pulled the window shut. Before turning off the lamp, she looked again at the professor, who lay stretched out beneath a blanket, and as she watched him his body shrank, as though the bed were a boat in motion, towing him into the distance. When she turned off the light, the bed seemed to drift. She was struck by the dreadful thought that, if she didn't go back over to him, the boat would sail even further into her husband's dreams.

6

The next time the ageing travel buddies got together for a trip was a little over a month after Professor Q's birthday.

Early that morning, Maria watched through the kitchen window as the sun rose to reveal a shimmering autumn cityscape. She smeared liberal quantities of thick, white sun lotion onto her arms while the professor sipped unhurriedly at his coffee, then raised the back of a metal teaspoon to the perfect dome of his boiled egg, knocking until a crack appeared in its shell. In an uncharacteristically whimsical tone, he told Maria that his limbs felt soft, as though bubbles were rising inside his bones. Maria frowned and suggested they make another visit to David's clinic, but he shook his head and tapped an index finger against a book lying on the breakfast table.

'Trust me,' he said, 'words are the best medicine.'

By the time Maria was ready to leave, he had vanished from the table. She scanned the room and discovered him in a living room armchair, spilling over its soft leather upholstery like a pile of wet mud; even his face seemed to have liquefied, its surface now rucked with waves. One of his hands dangled down the side of the chair, the palm curled into an operatic gesture, the book he had been reading now splayed on the floor. Maria went to pick it up, quickly identifying it as a work of contemporary fiction she had read during her university days. She turned to a page at random and felt exactly as she had all those years before, reading it for the first time: the author's convoluted vocabulary created a winding labyrinth, which made her feel that the safe, steady world around her had started to shake. Now, as she stood bathed in brilliant morning sunlight beside her sleeping husband, the effect of the densely printed words was even more powerful, like some kind of mysterious, nauseating spell.

Maria set off from the flat alone, walking poles in hand, sporting a baseball cap with a protective neck flap and a backpack equipped with water, a map, and a small guidebook to Nevers flora and fauna. Several years earlier, she had bought a full set of hiking equipment and started reading up on the ecology of the Nevers countryside. This was one of the many ways in which she was preparing for old age. Nevers was best known as a city, but in reality its developed areas were merely the embroidery along the skirt hem, and the vast majority of the territory was rugged mountains and unspoiled forests. Maria imagined all that lay waiting for her and Professor Q to discover: tucked-away villages, wetlands, lotus ponds, sprawling mountain ranges. More than enough to keep them both company for the rest of their days.

In past years, Professor Q had silently followed Maria and her friends on their hikes along Nevers mountain trails. Standing on the mountain peaks, looking down at the coastline far below, he would see the city skyscrapers transformed into innocent children's building blocks and, once again, the enduring beauty of it all would take his breath away. At the same time, thoughts would well up, unbidden, about the concealed paths linking Green Moss district to the city, paths used many years ago to smuggle in newcomers from the inland. He imagined those clandestine arrivals with stomachs growling from hunger, hiding in haystacks to evade police and their sniffer dogs. He imagined them shivering in the night-time dew, scared out of their wits at every new sound, not knowing if that stray rustle was an enormous boa constrictor closing in or just a timid little muntjac. When the fog was thick they would have lost their bearings, or worse their footing, plunging down hidden cliff faces.

To the north-east of Green Moss, in the tiny bay between Nevers and the Vanguard Republic, were the drowned bodies of the many unauthorized arrivals who had never arrived. Countless numbers had fled inland Ksana, planning to steal across the water to Nevers. They had stood on the shore and waited for night to fall, then leapt one after another into that sea of countless secrets, swimming desperately towards the other side, hoping to have delivered themselves across the border by morning. Even on windless, waveless nights, a swimmer who made the mistake of glancing back would inevitably discover travel companions vanished into blackness. Perhaps they had simply lost power, like toys with used-up batteries, or perhaps a shark had come and chewed off their legs, leaving them unable to propel themselves forward. Professor Q imagined their bodies sinking, hair fluttering like seaweed, eyes closed but ears open, as though still able to hear the voice of the sea.

He had heard that voice before. In fact, he knew it well. The sea was an enchanting beast that called out with every cell of its being, whispering sweet nothings in human ears. Sweet nothings except when it roared, unleashing a tongue that could drag whole boats into its belly in the blink of an eye. During the early days of his life in Nevers, after tidying up the seafood shop in the evening, Q would try and fail to clean the fishy ocean stench from between his fingers. Then he would set up his camp bed among piles of dried shrimp, dried scallops, and prickly black sea cucumbers beneath a ceiling hung with salted fish. He would lie there listening to the voice, and his little bed would rock with him as he tossed and turned through the night, leading him to believe that he was still on board the ship sailing from that remote southern country, heading for unknown land.

A pair of strong, rough hands had shoved him into the ship's hold. It was packed with wooden crates and cardboard boxes, some presumably for people, others for goods, but before he could look around properly someone had opened a small cardboard box and ordered him to get inside. He squeezed his bottom in first, then hugged his knees to his chest and forced his head between his thighs. Once the box was sealed he thought of magic shows he had seen, and he imagined that now, in the darkness, someone was casting a spell on him: all he had to do was keep quiet, resist the urge to pee, fart only very, very quietly, and he would exit the box a completely different person. Perhaps he would even fly into the sky like a dove! He didn't know what he would turn into, but out there in the pitch-black embrace of the ocean he felt his cramping legs start to crumble, until eventually they disappeared. This was why, when the magic box was finally opened and someone extended a hand to pull him onto shore, he didn't know how to follow their orders and *run for it.*

He still believed he must have run for it without any legs, all the way from that deserted beach into the city. That, or his physical body had entirely ceased to exist and he had made the journey as a ghost, blown in on the wind. Other people had been running with him but at some point they all left, and he was alone. Completely alone with regrown legs, walking down a sunny street. He saw dark-haired heads, piles of milky cabbages, flies circling slabs of blood-red meat, and the steely blurs of passing bicycles, but the only sound he heard was the sea—the sound of his own breathing, the sound of an absence of sound, which had been there in the darkness and which came again now to drown out everything else.

Someone in a green uniform with a gun at their waist slowed as they passed, clearly eyeing him, and he began to shiver. He knew about military uniforms, knew the thud of big uniform boots as they drew to a halt, knew about the look in soldiers' eyes. He had been enough places in his few short years to have seen that look many times before, and to know it was the look of a deporter. It meant a truncheon or a gun or some other weapon pointed at your nose, forcing you onto yet another boat. It could also mean a flimsy sheet of paper covered in foreign words, handed over like a practical joke: *A little proof of residence for you!*

On the Nevers mountain trails, Professor Q sometimes felt his legs disappear all over again. Sometimes he would be deep in thought, lagging behind the rest of the group, and knee-high grass would slice at his shins, causing him to lose sense of where he was. As the figures ahead of him shifted further into the distance, they felt more and more like total strangers. Soon enough Maria would look back, eyes squinted against the sun, and, noting her husband dithering at some far-off point along the ridge, she would wait for him to catch up. Professor Q would see her up ahead, but her outline was always hazy, and he could never make out the smile beaming from her face.

On this latest hike, when Maria looked back Professor Q wasn't there. The peak of her cap cast a long shadow over her face, and inside this shadow her brows furrowed with concern. Perhaps it had been unwise to leave her husband at home by himself. Lately, he seemed to have been sleeping for increasingly extended periods. He would fall silent during meals, his head bowed as though intently contemplating the cauliflower florets in his soup, and she would know he was sound asleep. In those moments he looked meek and innocent, and she clung to the sad yet at the same time consoling thought that andropause had come for him. Old age was nigh.

7

Maria was completely in the dark about how frequently her opinions diverged from those of her husband. Take his sleeping, for example. Professor Q did not believe napping more had anything whatsoever to do with his ageing body; it simply allowed him to spend more time dreaming. By the time Maria and her hiking pals had scaled their Nevers mountain peak and were standing five hundred metres above sea level, taking in the view, Professor Q had travelled along a dreamy pathway to somewhere even further away.

His first dreamland encounter was with a swarm of green bottle flies. After waving these buzzing irritations aside, he found himself amid a frenzy of lush tropical foliage. A magenta banana flower protruded from a cluster of bananas, the blossom pendulous and plump, like a cheerful penis. Scanning the undergrowth, he spotted a beady-eyed youngster inside a river, his dark, lanky body shaking like an aquatic plant with every gust of wind across the water. Professor Q smiled knowingly and the boy smiled with him, his grin rippling silently.

He knew why the boy was there. The boy had a ration coupon from his mother in his trouser pocket, but had decided not to head straight for the area with the military police. He wanted to avoid those men with guns at their waists, who would stop and search him however they saw fit, sizing up his genitals with the soles of their feet and snarling in his face with their big, gaping mouths. Instead he had struck out alone, heading in the opposite direction and wandering down to the river. As he stepped onto the little wooden bridge the locals had built across it, icy river water seeped into his good canvas shoes, but it didn't matter because his mind was on fire, and all he wanted was to get to the other side.

Young Q had no friends. Other boys claimed there was something girly about him, and they would giggle and press their noses into his neck, insisting he smelled like a woman. But Q didn't believe this was the real reason they avoided him. No, he had realized early on that he and his family simply didn't belong in that place in the far south, just as they hadn't belonged in any of the places where they had tried to live before.

Most families in those parts hung bright red flags above their doors, and when the flags opened in the wind, curved golden blades fluttered with them. There were no flags in young Q's home; there were intricate handwoven carpets and a ponderous, winding mode of speech. His elderly father spent most days pacing in front of the tattered books and magazines that were crammed into his bookshelves, pausing to pen long letters to unknown recipients. At dusk, he would sit beneath the banana tree in the garden and play mournful tunes on his harmonica. Meanwhile, Q's mother refused to comb her hair into a bun like the local women did, and she rejected their white blouses and mid-length skirts in favour of homemade floor-length dresses that clung to her generous buttocks, attracting a crowd of adolescent admirers every time she left the house.

Q was forbidden to roam the streets with other boys his age. He was supposed to stay inside and study. But when he brought home report cards, his father refused even to look up from whatever book he was reading, commenting simply: 'Best to forget what you learn at school.' Every day, Q would speak one language in class, only to come home and be forced to speak another. Sometimes he wished he could say nothing at all, could just crouch down and inspect ant trails all afternoon, but there was no getting around his father's insistence that he learn classical Ksanese poems by rote. His recitations always sounded furious.

In reality, he didn't enjoy interacting with his peers, especially not when they were smoking, or loitering on pavements to gawp at women. But he did enjoy following them, watching them climb gloomy narrow staircases, listening to the steps creak as they went. Sometimes women would lean out of upstairs windows to summon the boys up, crimson lips protruding enticingly from their shadowy profiles.

And what Q enjoyed above all else was going alone to filthy dive bars in the town centre, where blue- and green-eyed foreigners liked to gather. He had no idea where these foreigners came from: they were like soap bubbles, there briefly then gone. They made him think of his father, hiding in his study glued expectantly to the radio, as though waiting for some elusive piece of good news. The foreigners garbled their words and sounded just like those mysterious radio broadcasts, which even Q's father seemed to struggle to understand. Q tried his hardest to parse the foreigners' drunken speeches, using the few words he could recognize to guess at what was being said, before sauntering over and attempting to join in their conversations. Occasionally a meaty hand would reach down to pat him on the head, or someone would praise him extravagantly for his language skills, calling him their little buddy, their pal. In these moments tears sprang to his eyes, and he longed for his father to pass by and witness the scene.

This time, however, walking merrily across the bridge to the town centre, young Q wasn't thinking of the foreigners. He'd heard about a travelling theatre troupe performing out of a van, the stage hidden behind a pair of velvet curtains drawn across the back of the vehicle. He hadn't yet reached town, and had never seen the troupe perform, yet he felt as though he had—otherwise, how could he have predicted that the curtains would part to reveal a darkened stage full of puppets strung with transparent fishing line, their necks lolling uselessly to the side, as though hanged? Then the light bulbs around the edge of the stage came on, and the dead puppets leapt back to life. They were dressed like gaudy European courtiers and all of them, male and female alike, fluttered long thick eyelashes around big doe-like eyes. Music blasted onto the stage, and they started to dance. Their heads spun like carousel lanterns, turning a full 360 degrees, one moment whirling pigtails, the next pink-daubed cheeks.

'And now for the striptease!'

The song came to an end and only two puppets remained on stage, each wearing a crown. They held hands and squealed with delight.

The audience held their breath. The dancing was a little stiff, but no one had ever seen a striptease before and they were mesmerized by the gyrating puppet bodies and the tiny doll clothes being peeled off one item at a time—robes, belts, stockings. The puppets kept going until all their clothes were off, revealing their bodies to be nothing more than a few crudely assembled blocks of wood. Even then, the audience remained entranced. The puppets dropped their jaws and cackled at each other, then pulled off what turned out to be wigs with toy crowns stuck on top. There was no longer any denying that they were just two blank wooden shapes with nothing left to tell them apart—

'May they live happily ever after!'

The audience booed and hissed. Only Q seemed to notice the director peeking out from the wings, one eye filmy and tinged with blue, like the cross section of a preserved egg, but his smile full of mischief.

When had Q seen all this? He couldn't remember, and neither could he remember why the director had singled him out after the show. He had been standing in the audience, one hand still in his trouser pocket clinging anxiously to his mother's ration coupon. The director had grabbed his free hand and shoved it into a grubby hemp pouch.

'Time for our special feature!'

The director was holding up a Ghost Leg lottery board with colourful gambling chips stuck all over it. The chips followed limb-like lines down the board, heading for unknown prizes at the bottom.

'You will get what you truly desire.'

Q felt his hand withdraw from his pocket, relinquishing the hot, damp coupon to the director. Inside the pouch, his other hand opened wide.

'What do you feel?'

Q frowned. Inside that tiny goodie bag, he felt something alive. He dared not say it aloud, but it was a body, many times bigger than the bag. He was touching a stiff, well-defined part of it, something like a statue, but at the same time it was a whole world, cloudlike in its softness.

'Give it another go.'

The director seemed to see everything. Q reached even deeper, knowing as he did so that he was getting close to the body's most secret of places. How strange that there was nothing hard sticking up. How strange that this body wasn't scorching hot like his was.

'Now what do you feel?'

'I feel something, but it's not what I want,' Q replied, blushing furiously.

They both knew he was lying. Q screwed his eyes shut, and the director's good eye roved the twisted contours of his face.

The director seemed to assume Q was in the throes of ecstasy, but it wasn't like that. As Q tried to push his fingers even deeper, to the absolute limits of that mysterious realm, he found there was nothing there. All he felt was a place where something had been torn off. He realized that the body in the pouch was his own body, and that an unknown hand had crashed in from outside and was now wrenching him open, invading his deepest, most secret parts.

He snatched his hand back, terrified. Without even pausing to see what lucky gift he might have pulled out, he turned and fled.

The road before him was unfamiliar. He appeared to have entered an even deeper region of his dream. Giant tropical plants dwarfed him, shrinking him to the size of a miniature figurine. He searched frantically for a way forward, pushing through tree trunks spread like veins, and leaves that sliced painfully at his skin. He walked briefly along a narrow, stony path, but soon found it impossibly overgrown with weeds. Then came a rustling that he at first mistook for a hare, until the undergrowth parted to reveal a girl. She had long hair hanging loose past her shoulders, and her body was small and delicate (although still many times larger than his). Without saying a word, she unbuttoned her top, letting it fall open to expose her right breast.

Q stared, joy coursing through his body. He had never seen such an enormous, full, looming breast before. He tried to walk closer, but found he couldn't move. He was trapped inside a chalk circle drawn on the ground, a trick his father used to play to punish him for not coming home at night: a cursed border. But crossing it wouldn't be difficult, surely—wasn't his father old and frail now? Hadn't he long since slunk off to a faraway land? As though performing an exorcism, and without any real idea what he might be saying, Q yelled foreign-sounding words. They didn't work; he remained stuck. And though he hated to admit it, he was frightened: the girl's lips were tightly sealed but her breast was ferocious, furious, an angry tiger disturbed in the forest. Then there were the veins, extending from the nipple like emerald streams, and all he wanted was to touch them. That livid red nipple was so close! Why couldn't he reach it?

The world was pasted like a magic mirror over the face of the young Q. Professor Q realized now he could see everything in it so much more clearly than when he was actually young. He shivered. The sun was setting. He gazed down at his protruding belly and the chubby little appendage below it, nestled against his thighs like a sleepy pet, still warm from the last rays of sunlight.

He went into the bathroom, feeling as if he were still the young boy from his dream, weighed down by the old man he had to carry with him. It infuriated him to think that the boy's face had been stolen, replaced by one with morose parallel lines etched between the brows, its cheeks collapsed into sagging jowls, and on top of which thinning grey hair lay limply against the scalp. He brought his dream eyes to the mirror, contemplating the version of himself inside it. His irises were not so dark brown as he had thought: ringed around the outside was the faintest hint of foreigner blue. The foreign-eyed man in the mirror stared deeply into Professor Q's eyes.

The wall clock ticked like a bomb, seeming to keep time with Professor Q's pounding heart rate. He suddenly remembered Maria and the rest of the group, out somewhere on a Nevers mountain trail, and thought contentedly of how far away they were from him. He might have been a little older than most of them in years, but he hadn't aged in the same way they had. There had been a painful moment at a recent gathering, when a divorce lawyer called Mr C had exclaimed that he and Professor Q were twins. The group was out for dinner, and this Mr C had laughed so heartily at his own joke that Professor Q had been able to see all the green vegetable matter caught between his teeth. It had certainly not escaped his notice that they were wearing identical sweaters.

Maria had bought him the sweater. How best to describe its

colour? The first time he saw it, it had called to mind a carefully arranged, cellophane-wrapped, odourless dog turd, and he was unsure why he'd ever agreed to the terrible burden of wearing it. Now, all his suppressed resentment over the incident came rushing back to the surface. He strode vengefully into the bedroom and upended the ten-inch-thick mattress on the bed frame, dismantling the interlocking, detachable slats beneath it. Before reaching the decades-old belongings festering below, he was hit with the thrilling stink of camphor.

A sky-blue ruffled shirt and a black sheepskin jacket were the first treasures to come to light (he could already see Maria's disapproving frown). There was no need to try them on: he knew they would no longer fit. But among the piles of old clothes, he uncovered a fedora he had bought years earlier, on a trip abroad. It was squashed flat from the weight of everything above it but, to his surprise, it popped back into its former, elegant shape in almost no time at all.

The hat was charcoal grey with a black band. If he put it on and tilted it just so, he found that it completely hid his thinning hair, and cast most of his face in shadow. As though tugged by an invisible thread, his mouth slowly curled up at one corner. No one, not even he, would notice the sorrowful creases in his forehead now. The clock ticked menacingly, reminding him that time was running out. He had to hurry! It felt like a momentous decision: he would put on the fedora and set off for Valeria Island to catch the show with Aliss and the magician.

8

Autumn was Nevers at its most magnificent. The subtropical humidity temporarily abated, the sky was exaggeratedly blue, and murky soil-dwelling creatures re-emerged on glistening trails. Even the monotonous, overcrowded apartment blocks looked fresh and energetic in the wheat-gold light. But the dry air crackled with mysterious sparks, and all it took was one inopportune gust of wind to set a mountaintop on fire. Maria and her friends were spared any such flames but after a whole day's hiking—a whole day of fording slippery mountain streams and wading through reedy marshes—they were on their way back down when Maria missed a step and twisted her ankle.

Her cheeks burned as her friends rushed her to a viewing platform bench, urging her to rest. She was an experienced hiker and knew the sprain had only happened because her thoughts had been elsewhere. It shocked her to realize she might not be as independent as she liked to think: without her husband by her side, she had been unable to keep her mind off him.

She looked at the couples arrayed before her in their immaculate hiking outfits, anxious little smiles on their faces, and she thought back to private get-togethers with the wives during which they chattered on about their husbands' dalliances with other women. Usually they would talk and talk and then dissolve into furious tears, but sometimes it was as if they were discussing a plot point from a racy soap opera, and they would end up doubled over, laughing. Maria never said much. Sooner or later the conversation would turn to her own situation, and the women would lavish her with praise, declaring her husband the most faithful man on the planet.

At these moments, Maria struggled to contain a smile. She would never have admitted it to anyone, but this halo-granting was always her favourite part. It was also true: she had never once had reason to doubt her husband's fidelity. From the day they married, he had always been home by the time she finished work. At her behest, they were careful with money, and certainly didn't waste it on hiring an overseas domestic worker to help around the house. If they ate dinner at home, she did the cooking (she had strict ideas about nutrition and refused to entrust the task to anyone else) and afterwards Professor Q washed up. She would gladly have shared such tips for a happily married life with the other women, but their attention spans were short and they were easily distracted by a luxury silk scarf or a new, limited-edition designer handbag. Maria had no interest in such things, though what she detested most was when the women had a glass of wine or two too many and started getting loose-tongued about their sex lives, coming out with distasteful stories, exclaiming, 'On his last business trip, he was away so long there wasn't even time for him to get his shoes off after he came through the front door . . .'

On the viewing platform bench, her face devoid of make-up, Maria looked luminously beautiful. In the eyes of the attendant husbands, she was as divine as the Virgin Mary, or Guanyin, or an innocent schoolgirl. They felt their blood rise in her presence, even if they knew better than to say anything. If Professor Q had been there, they could at least have satisfied their cravings vicariously, probing him with questions, trying to crack the eternal mystery of how he had scored such a goddess for a wife. Even when Professor Q was present, however, his answer never wavered. 'I was chosen,' he said, over and over again.

The more a sentence is repeated, the greater the space it comes to occupy in one's memory, and the harder it is to tell whether or not it has any basis in fact. Professor Q was convinced Maria had first appeared in his life as a voice. He couldn't remember what she had said, only that he had never before heard such lucid, elegant, perfectly spoken Valerian. It was even more perfect than the Valerian of those professors who actually came from Valeria! Q was a student at the time, older than most of his peers, and he spent his days studying all alone in the Lone Boat University library. Until, that is, the afternoon Maria's voice was delivered into his ears like a message from God. Her words combined vowels and consonants in such an exquisite way, and contained such gorgeous modulations of pitch, that they became musical compositions—or, no, better put: they formed perfect silver beads, seemingly aimed directly at him. By that stage in his life Q had learned at least four languages, but with all of them he felt little more than a trained parrot. No matter which language he was speaking, he was convinced that, to a careful listener, he sounded as though his mouth were full of pebbles; there was always that lingering trace of a foreign accent. He knew he would never speak Valerian as impeccably as the voice in the library.

It was when he went searching for the source of the voice that he first laid eyes on Maria. She was sitting in a narrow, straight-backed chair with her knees demurely together, engrossed in a thick dictionary. She wore a dress that shielded her body like a nun's habit, its buttons sealing her closed. Her scraped-back hair was neat and shiny, but her fringe seemed to fall across her brow in complete defiance of any prevailing trend, giving it the impression of having fallen outside of time itself, and therefore of being eternal. To Q, this became a totem, overshadowing all other aspects of Maria's appearance.

It was like a key that slid right into some peculiar mechanism in his brain, fastening the two of them together.

'That is the most impressive Valerian I have ever heard.'

Maria looked up, apparently not shy at all. Clearly, she was a girl accustomed to praise from strangers, well aware of her talents. She nodded briefly and then, like an examiner announcing a grade, she said: 'Your Valerian isn't bad either.'

Now she was observing Q intently. He was noticeably older than she was, with wild, unkempt hair. He was also painfully thin, as though suffering from long-term malnourishment.

A crease flickered between Maria's eyebrows.

'Yours could be just as good as mine,' she said. 'Would you like to practise together?'

Q and Maria practised Valerian together in the library, on benches in the park, and on strolls around the university lake. Most of the time Q was silent, listening to Maria's mellifluous Valerian as she told him the story of her life. As it turned out, she had grown up entirely in Nevers and never once set foot in Valeria; her accent came from a lifetime of radio listening. From when she was very young, she had tuned in to a colonizer radio service that broadcast round-the-clock classical music and Valerian news. (It still existed, although the number of its listeners was greatly reduced.) Maria was a law student, and Q came to understand that her elegant mode of speech and exceptional grades went hand in hand with a strictly ordered vision of the world. In her eyes, everything could be categorized. The judge stood in the judge's stand, the witness on the witness stand. The criminally insane were sent to asylums, criminals to jail. Every person and every thing had a proper place to which it could (and should) be consigned.

One day Maria looked into Q's eyes and said, half-jokingly, 'You don't look like you're from Nevers. Where are you really from?'

Q couldn't tell if Maria saw him trembling, but he did notice that this girl who never smiled was offering him a tentative smile for the very first time.

It was a balmy afternoon, and Maria had showed up at Q's dormitory building with a bag of oranges. They were the only two people in the lobby. By this stage in their acquaintance they had stopped speaking so much; language no longer held such importance. Q focused less on Maria's accent and enunciation and more on the delicate pink of her lips, the graceful curve of her neck when she inclined her head, the way her skirt billowed tantalizingly around her calves as she cycled. In all his life leading up to this point, Q had never once been intimate with a woman. Now, he would let his finger fall gently in the space between Maria's neck and shoulders. He would stand behind her and inhale deeply in the vicinity of her ears. His body was telling her everything he needed to say—could she really not hear him? He had written her a poem and given it to her tucked inside a notebook, but he had no idea whether anything he wrote had affected her. When she handed back the notebook a few days later, she had merely covered the poem in grammatical corrections and comments on places where his similes fell short of logic.

In the dormitory lobby, Q spoke in hushed tones of his plans for graduate school, informing Maria he would soon be leaving Nevers.

They were sitting side by side on a bench. Q had hoped Maria would say something in response to his grand announcement, but instead she picked out an orange from her bag and opened it reverently, as though it were a gift. Each fleshy segment of the exposed fruit was flawless, carefully packaged within its own delicate membrane. Maria peeled away a segment and placed it in her mouth, piercing it with her neat white teeth. Its fragrance filled Q's nostrils, and he felt his appetite vanish. His palms were sweating. He didn't know what to do with his hands. Maria turned to look at him, smiling, but the smile soon faded. They would both go on to remember it as a balmy afternoon during which nothing in particular had happened.

After Q left Nevers, he and Maria started writing to each other, exchanging news in Valerian. Maria told him about her seamless transition to a high-level government post. She told him about a typhoon that smashed in all her office windows. She told him about an evening she had been walking home alone, along a path they had often walked together, when she stumbled upon what she first took for a cluster of mice, but which turned out to be newborn kittens. She told him that every evening after work she would feed the kittens leftovers from her lunch. She told him that the kittens were no longer kittens. She told him that she hadn't been able to find them in the usual place and had eventually spotted them up a tree, looking like a flock of birds about to take flight.

Q replied to every one of her letters. What did he say? The moment he posted a letter, he would forget. All he remembered was that he hadn't told her how he truly felt, and as a result his letters were always stylistically brilliant but lacking in substance. Even when he finally received his doctorate and returned to Nevers as the newly greying Professor Q, he still couldn't bring himself to tell Maria about how, for all those years, whether in his Nevers university dormitory or his Valeria university student halls, he would listen to other people's bed frames creaking through the wall. The noise would slow and speed up again, mixing with plaintive female moans. He wished he could get closer to the source of the sound, but all he had were his own skinny fingers and the blank, unresponsive ceiling bearing down on him from above.

Maria's distant voice had acted as a kind of legal mandate, commanding him to keep his virginity intact. Meanwhile, with the intensity of an A-grade student let loose on a homework assignment, he dedicated himself to researching the art of heterosexual lovemaking, watching porn of every possible variety in the hope that, one day, he would be able to put all his theory into practice.

Toasting guests at his wedding banquet, his face gleaming red, he had been in high spirits. No one could tell, but inside the trousers of his crisply ironed wedding suit, his pubic hair was fresh and neat, trimmed the morning before into a little Charlie Chaplin–style moustache. Observing his handiwork in the mirror, he had been delighted to note that the effect was just as his books had promised: his penis really did look thicker.

After such a long wait, Professor Q was used to being patient. He had planned to begin his wedding-night activities by giving Maria a full-body massage, but things got off to an unpromising start when she came into the bedroom wearing a long white nightdress and lay down stiffly on the bed, looking more like a patient awaiting a medical examination than a bride. As soon as he touched her, she began to giggle uncontrollably. He became flustered and lost track of his massage, poking her seemingly at random, which only made her giggle harder. He decided to climb directly on top of her and try to kiss her, because at least that would put a stop to the giggling, but instead it made things even worse. The following day he attempted to show her an enlightening video, but after only a few minutes she was already screaming and covering her eyes, ordering him to turn it off.

On the seventh evening of their married life, Maria came into the living room after her bath and waited for her husband to come and practise kissing and caressing her, as he had done every other night so far. This time, however, he didn't appear. When Maria finally entered the bedroom to see what was keeping him, she found him stretched across the bed, deep in his dreams, and she felt distinctly as if she had lost something.

Unbeknownst to Maria, her husband was happily ogling another her in his dreams. This Maria had long, flowing hair and was standing by a half-open window, gazing into the distance. The professor was captivated by the glorious curve where her bottom met her lower back. She didn't turn around, but in a warm, maternal voice she said, 'Don't you want to come closer?'

He nodded and shoved his head under her skirt, burying his face in her warm, round buttocks.

What a pity Maria couldn't see what went on behind her husband's forehead! Had she been able to, she would have discovered that, over the course of their long marriage, she made frequent appearances in his dreams, in a variety of guises. For example, one night he dreamt of a nauseating odour. When he entered the kitchen, he discovered one of his Marias stirring a cauldron of pea soup. Every so often Maria would go to the local farmers' market and come home with a large sack of organic peas, which she proceeded to turn into soup. She had no idea how much her husband loathed the stink the soup made while it boiled, and detested its horrible, frog-green hue, its revoltingly thick texture, the feeling of all the unchewable pea skins catching in his throat when he swallowed. How was he supposed to tell her? When she set a bowl of it in front of him, he never said a word. Forcing down a bowl of soup felt infinitely more possible than opposing his wife. It had been that way since their first meeting: she opened her mouth and he was powerless to resist, his educated parrot tongue no use at all.

In another dream, he encountered a Maria seated at a piano, wearing her wedding veil. How he gave thanks! Now, at last, shielded by those most banal, commonplace, repeatedly uttered of vows, he could march boldly to the lacy hem of her gown and she would no longer be able to accuse him of lechery. Her feet were bare, cheerfully so, and those wriggling, liberated toes seemed to have something to tell him. He felt like a blushing bride about to enter a church and, in this version of events, Maria was the church: *Ask, and it shall be given you; seek, and ye shall find; knock, and it shall be opened unto you; for every one that asketh, receiveth; and he that seeketh findeth; and to him that knocketh it shall be opened.*

'Do you?' he whispered in her ear.

He heard Maria laugh, the sound quiet but resonant, echoing

from all corners of the house like the silvery pealing of angels. How could there be so many Marias? Which one was the real her? From behind him, one of them spoke:

'Didn't you know she has no ears? She can't hear you. She doesn't have lips either, so how could she answer?'

He went to embrace the Maria in the wedding dress, feeling like an awkward child. He stared desperately into her eyes, as though expecting them to be transparent, allowing him to see into that Maria's body to the real Maria hiding inside it. But all he could see was a reflection of the world, which, in a way that he couldn't understand, seemed to have sealed shut a vitally important door (a door that cannot be opened will always seem the most vitally important of doors).

The various Marias assembled before him and snatched the wedding-dress Maria from his hands. Then they stripped her— first her veil, then her necklace, her gown, her underwear, continuing until they could set her on the dining table like an exhibit (or perhaps an icon) and her whole, flawless body was displayed before him. To his profound surprise, Maria's body was truly a shrine, a sealed entity, a church with no door through which to enter.

9

Let us now return to that early autumn evening a few months after Professor Q's birthday. Maria stood up from the bench where she had been resting her ankle and continued down the mountain, chatting and joking with her friends. Meanwhile, Professor Q was back once again on the Valeria Island antiques street.

The street was strangely deserted. A solitary figure in a long overcoat hurried past him like a character from a silent film. Professor Q could see the shophouse in the distance; it was on a corner, and he recognized the distinctive curve of its first-storey overhang. The performance advertised on the flyer was not even supposed to have started yet, but as he drew closer he saw that the noticeboard had gone from the ground floor, along with the display window behind it. In its place was a locked iron gate covered in droplet-shaped fretwork, each droplet gaping at him like an empty eye socket.

He turned back to the street. Where was everyone? The road was open to traffic, but not a car was in sight. He stepped into the middle of the road and saw, much further down, a clown juggling small red balls. The clown started to smile, his mouth widening until it seemed to take over his entire face. Then he lost track of his juggling and the balls fell from the air, bouncing off his body and rolling along the ground. He beckoned to Professor Q. (Or did he? There still didn't seem to be anyone else around.) When Professor

Q failed to move, the clown threw up his hands and whizzed over at great speed, travelling on what turned out to be roller skates. Drawing to a halt, he then turned to the shophouse and pointed insistently at a spot to one side of the gate, where the professor now saw there was a metal umbrella rack. It was not yet rainy season but the rack was filled with umbrellas—and weren't they, somehow, a little too tidy? As if sensing the professor's hesitation, the clown winked, twitching the big silver star painted over his right eye, and then fell into a deep bow, as though to say: *Help yourself.*

The clown looked familiar, although Professor Q couldn't think where he might have seen him before. After a moment's hesitation, he tried to take an umbrella, only to find the one he had chosen was extraordinarily heavy. It wouldn't budge from its place on the rack. The clown shook his head and contorted his mouth into a dramatic upside-down U, pretending to cry. Summoning a wave of righteous anger, imagining himself King Arthur pulling the sword from the stone, Professor Q tried again with different umbrellas. They were all stuck fast. When he eventually reached one that slid out easily, he had built up to yanking with such force that he lost his balance, and would have fallen backwards had the clown not been there to catch him. A second later, the clown started gesturing for him to step through the now wide-open gate, its opening mechanism apparently activated by the removal of the umbrella. The only thing on the other side was a narrow staircase, plunging downwards. Professor Q glanced over the edge and felt a wave of vertigo.

Was Aliss down there? The thought scared him but, at the same time, there was something enticing about the darkness swirling beneath his feet. As the gate closed behind him, he gripped the handrail and stepped gingerly into the void. The steps seemed endless; it was impossible to see how many were left to go. Just as he was starting to panic, he found himself in a corridor. The corridor connected to another corridor, and then another after that. He had lived in

Nevers for decades and was well aware that buildings kept growing taller, relegating bookshops and cafés to higher and higher floors, but he had no idea anyone had started to develop the space underground. It was too dim to see clearly, but he could hear the faint sound of machinery in motion.

A light blinked on, revealing both sides of the corridor to be covered in snaking pipes, feeding into tanks of varying sizes. A complex system of cocks and valves seemed to be controlling the water flow. Mechanisms were activated, gears spun. A clock started ticking, a bird sprang from the wall, an owl slid across the ceiling. Beneath the clock, a pendulum clanked back and forth. Water poured out of an open pipe at the end of the corridor, forming a little river. A tiny clockwork boat bobbed along it while a musician the size of a thumb paced the deck playing a tiny violin.

Professor Q found he had reached an empty room, its floor covered with chequerboard tiles. In the far corner of the room was a grand piano, its keys dipping and rising by themselves, accompanying the violin music.

He followed the river across the room to a doorway on the other side, screened off by two velvet curtains. He brought both hands to the curtain join and parted the fabric to make a spyhole, just large enough to peek at what was happening on the other side. An enormous crystal chandelier hung from a high, vaulted ceiling. Up there in the arches, he saw men and women in opera masks and sumptuous evening attire, brocade fabrics glinting slyly, fox fur stoles and overcoats whirling about their bodies. A moment later, he realized these figures were reflections of guests assembled in a grand banqueting hall below. The air smelled of exhaled wine, and waiters in tailcoats and bunny ears circulated with big silver trays. Dotted among the crowd were oversized music boxes and mechanical dolls. Silver discs spun in intricate wood cases, skulls danced, peacocks spouted water from their backsides.

Professor Q's attention was drawn to a wall of tinted glass, the kind used in aquariums to separate fish from viewers. Rather than fish, however, the glass shielded a collection of naked human figures, some sitting, others standing, all of them frozen in place. They were stiff, not moving at all, yet he detected a flicker of something lifelike behind their features. And very soon he had discovered among their ranks one pale body in particular.

He first saw her back, her spine like a giant millipede extending from her coccyx to her neck. Her legs were bent into two beautiful triangles, and she hugged them to her chest like a resting ballet dancer, her head between her knees. Professor Q drifted helplessly towards the glass. He placed his hands against its icy surface and stared, transfixed: she was not sitting, as he had thought, but lying inside a case turned on its side, the open end facing him. If the case had been upright, she would have looked like a curled foetus. He wanted to see more, to look longer at the purple veins faintly visible beneath that delicate skin, but then the lights went out and her body vanished into darkness.

Several spotlights focused on a stage, illuminating a European soldier pinned down by a tiger. The tiger was snarling, its claws sunk deep into the soldier's uniform and its mouth wide, as if about to tear into the soldier's neck; the soldier was moaning and swinging one arm helplessly back and forth. Both were carved from wood but their respective cries sounded soulful and alive, sending the audience wild with excitement. Things continued like this for some time, until a mechanism was activated and the circular base rotated, revealing another side to the struggle.

On this side, the soldier's body had already been mauled, the skin and flesh torn away to expose his breastbone and internal organs. The soldier and the tiger were silent now. A magician stepped out from the wings, his face half-obscured by a black mask behind which his eyes glinted emerald green. He took a deep bow and then approached the tiger. Extending a white-gloved hand, he opened up its flank and began to play a rousing European victory march. The stage revolved once again, continuing until the audience could see that the tiger's body had been concealing two rows of copper pipes, and that the magician's fingers were dancing along a line of white keys. When the song was over, the magician snatched his hands away, turned, bowed again, and the lights went up to instant, thunderous applause.

The magician went to stand at a podium. He produced a gavel, which he proceeded to bang three times, and everyone in the hall scrambled to hold up white cards with numbers written on them. It dawned on Professor Q that this was an auction, and that the printed brochures everyone was holding were auction catalogues. Suddenly conscious of his casual attire, he pulled the brim of his hat lower over his face and slunk into a corner. Judging by the cheers, the tiger-versus-soldier fight scene must have sold. The lights dimmed again, readying, he assumed, for the next item.

The hall filled with Tchaikovsky's *Swan Lake*. From within the shadow of his hat, the professor kept his eyes on the stage. Now, the only figure up there was a ballerina and, once again, he recognized her immediately. Aliss was wearing a swan headpiece and a cream-coloured ballet costume, the bodice tight and the tutu rippling around her waist like a leaf of lettuce. A second, smaller stage had appeared on the original stage, in the form of a wooden case: Aliss stood on top of it with one leg up behind her head, her arms in the wide V of an open fan.

Professor Q realized that Aliss's case was an enormous music box. It was divided into three layers, the top one being her usual hiding place; now that the box lid was opened, this top layer had become her stage. The layer below this dance floor was covered in glass, through which he could see a gleaming golden roller rotating against the teeth of a musical comb, music tinkling out like a stream of water. Aliss raised her chin and began to turn, speeding up until she was whipping round and round like a tornado. Then she started to leap about, her toes shooting through the air with arrow-like precision. She was flying across the stage, moving with all the agility of a bird, yet even at her fastest point Professor Q had the impression her gaze remained unwaveringly on him.

Her movements slowed with the music, until she stopped completely. She folded her wings and lay down on the floor, eyes still on the professor. The colour of her irises seemed to change, and he felt a spike of fear in the pit of his stomach. There was a long pause, after which the audience started to clap and he realized the performance was over: Aliss had lost power. The magician reappeared from the shadows, picked her up by the waist, and put her back on the top layer of the music box, as though packing away a violin. Then he closed the box, turning the key ninety degrees to the left, then another ninety degrees to the left, until the lock clicked. Now all Aliss would see was darkness.

Was the magician going to auction Aliss? He banged once again with his gavel and the room calmed into whispers, but not a single person raised their card. The magician waited and then banged a couple more times, until the room fell silent. Then, in faltering Valerian, he began to speak:

'Like most of you, because of various reasons, I left the place of my birth and came to Nevers. Now, I have lived here for half of my life. Reluctantly, I must inform you today of the bad news that I have decided to close my antiques shop and return to the homeland of my ancestors.'

He waited for the crowd to quieten down, then continued:

'But I have also good news! As you know, Aliss is the crown jewel of the shop and has never been for sale. But today I must leave her here in Nevers forever more. And so, before this auction is over, I will give her as a gift to one lucky member of this audience.'

72

Instantly, everyone was excitedly murmuring into one another's ears, the volume in the room mounting until the magician banged his gavel yet again.

'Who will get her, you ask? Ha! Fate has already decided. Now I ask you all to look at your right palms. Do you see a cross? Whoever sees a cross is our lucky winner!'

Nobody had drawn anything on Professor Q's palm but he still found himself opening his right hand to check. It was aged and wrinkly, the palm lined with bewildering creases, but other than those there was nothing there. As he inspected the creases, a spotlight seemed to detonate over his head, flooding him with light. Everyone in the hall spun around to stare at him, including the magician. The magician brought his mouth to the microphone and his voice boomed through the hall:

'Raise your palm!'

'There's nothing there,' Professor Q shouted back.

'Nothing there? Has not the Good Lord left his mark upon your palm?'

Before the professor could take a second look, music started to play and the lights went down. How did he get on stage? When did Aliss put her hand in his? She pulled him to her and placed his hands on her waist. Then, held between his palms, she began to spin. Aliss was spinning so quickly that he couldn't make out any part of her face, but still he felt enveloped in her all-encompassing gaze. She eventually slowed, then turned away from him and swept a leg in an arc through the air, hooking it around his back. He couldn't see her face but he could feel the curves of her back and bottom pressing against his body. This doll was so soft, her body softer than that of any 'real' woman he had ever encountered. He wished they could stay there in that pose forever but, in a flash, Aliss was dancing again. Who knows how he knew to do it, but he found himself holding her aloft, her legs stretched wide. When she landed, his hands went back to her waist. He was behind her again, her head blocking his line of vision, and he could hear applause pouring in from all sides. He felt flustered, unsure whether to let go of Aliss or to keep holding the position. Was it even really him up there with her?

The magician was back. He forced his head in between Professor Q and Aliss, bringing his lips so close to the professor that for a moment it seemed he might kiss him.

'Now you must answer one simple question and Aliss will be yours!' he proclaimed, his breath hot against Professor Q's face.

Then he extricated himself and continued with his speech:

'Come, with the Lord God as our witness, do you—who are you? I don't even know your name!—do you, whoever you are, accept Aliss into your home? Out there in the world of humans, will you acknowledge her existence, her being another species entirely, and do you take her, for richer or for poorer, for better or for worse, in sickness and in health . . . do you, my good gentleman, do you?'

With his hands still on Aliss's waist, Professor Q had the feeling this was a wedding, except he couldn't see his bride.

'You have ten seconds. Tell me, do you?'

The only sound in the hall was the ticking of a clock. *Ten, nine, eight, seven, six, five, four, three, two, one.* Was time moving forwards or backwards? Aliss's waist vanished, then her beautiful bottom, then her legs. Professor Q's hands were grasping at air. He raised his right one; there was no single 'X' on his palm, instead there were layers and layers of Xs, covering the whole of its surface.

10

It didn't snow during Nevers winters, but there were always a few romantic days when the city was blanketed in thick, snowlike smog. It erased the mountain range and made the towering city buildings seem as meek and peaceful as hibernating animals, huddling sleepily together while cars blundered around at their feet. Every year, the smog grew thicker. You could tell by simply extending a hand, with no need for any official government report, but this was an age in which you couldn't trust what was right in front of you. Newspapers and televisions maintained there was no smog in Nevers, or else that there had always been smog in Nevers, and that these were two sides of the same truth. And no matter which side a person chose to believe, the important thing was that the pollution could not possibly have blown in from inland Ksana; the important thing was that the construction of the high-speed rail connection and the cross-harbour bridge could not possibly have resulted in any kind of negative impact on the Nevers ecology.

Consider Maria, at work inside a 101-storey government office block in Lion Slope. The building was less than two years old and, on the day under consideration, it had been consumed by smog. Maria was in her office on the eighty-first floor, the curtains wide open, the city outside vanished into a vast blankness that, despite what you might think, she actually found soothing.

Her department had originally been housed in a colonial building in the western part of Valeria Island. At just over ten storeys high, that building had not been tall, but it had been situated on top of a mountain, with a clear view to the cars and pedestrians on the road winding up to it. When the department moved into its custom-built skyscraper, the first thing Maria noticed was the change in view. From that great height she could no longer make out people or traffic on the streets below, because the streets now blended into an untouchable dark morass from which all sound was extinguished. Any time she approached the window, she was seized by a terror of stepping out onto thin air.

While the building was still under construction, Maria had heard more than one rumour of a worker falling off it.

Happened right here.

Here one minute, gone the next.

At least two of them, apparently.

A crane broke down and the man inside tried to climb out onto the building, but he slipped.

Soon after the move in, Maria noticed two of the cleaning staff gesticulating towards her office window. She went over, intending to ask what was going on, but they started and rushed off, nodding and smiling weakly.

She decorated her new office with a succulent plant and a goldfish in a small tank, which she kept on her desk. Despite these efforts, the room still felt empty. The goldfish would flick its tail and she would sense something ghostly and unsettling out of the corner of her eye.

She started to realize that colleagues had disappeared in the move, and that the faces and uniforms of security guards and cleaning staff had changed. Miss M the accountant had vanished, along with several clerks. It was as if they had never been there at all. At the first interdepartmental meeting in the new location, Maria was shocked to discover that even department heads had been replaced. Among the new appointees was a transfer from inland Ksana, who was chairing the meeting. Affairs proceeded more or less as usual, although Maria felt that everybody present was quieter than before, seemingly without any queries about the latest proposals. Even more concerning was that several items on the meeting agenda were not proposals at all but announcements, made without any prior discussion. With each new statement from the chair, the room erupted into applause, and Maria felt she had no choice but to join in, smiling and clapping fervently along with everyone else.

If she could have spoken about these private doubts of hers with a trusted colleague or two, perhaps that would have helped her to understand what was going on. The problem was, the department had transformed into a foreign land overnight. She couldn't risk talking about sensitive department policy with newer members of staff, especially as they were unlikely to know any more about it than she did. Instead, she decided to focus on winning their trust and support. Now, more than at any other point in her life, Maria began to pay careful attention to how she behaved in the office.

One day, out of the blue, she received an email that seemed to have been sent in error: neither the subject line nor the contents had anything to do with her work. It contained a city-planning map of Nevers, providing an urban planner's projection of the city in twenty years' time. Nevers was simply sketched out and filled with brightly coloured blocks, like a child's jigsaw puzzle. This version of Nevers looked unfamiliar, not only because more land reclamation projects had altered the coastline and new islands had appeared in the sea, but also because the city districts themselves had been redrawn. Several districts had vanished entirely. The neighbourhood where she and Professor Q had bought their flat remained, but many of the poorest areas and those with high concentrations of retirement homes had been cleanly excised (where had they put all those people?). And all those lotus ponds, mountain trails, and mangrove swamps that she planned to spend her retirement exploring with her husband had been replaced by business hubs and high-end residential estates. In Green Moss district, the land currently occupied by Lone Boat University had become a scientific research centre!

Maria had not heard any news of Lone Boat closing down. If the map was actually representative of city plans to be carried out within the next twenty years, surely many of those projects would be about to start? Or, in fact, would need to have done so already. And how could the government start without having made the plans public? The prospective Nevers outlined on the map filled Maria with dread; refusing to look at it any longer, she deleted the whole email. The map had been marked as confidential and was clearly sent to her in error, thus she would stick to the office code of conduct and get rid of it. What a relief to have this code! It made it easy for her to reach a decision, because the decision was not hers to make. To discuss this kind of matter with a colleague, or even an uninitiated husband or friend, could lead to consequences beyond her control. If she could have pushed a button to delete the map from her own memory, she would have done so without a moment's hesitation. That way, at least her meticulously planned retirement years would not be overshadowed by the spectre of what she had seen on the map.

Maria picked up her thermos and left her desk. To reach the staff tea room, she had to pass through an open-plan work area. The desks were screened off, but with partitions low enough that she could still see clearly what each employee was up to. Today, they were either focused on their computer screens or holding work discussions on their phones. When they saw Maria, they all sat up straight and nodded deferentially. She hoped they didn't think she was policing them. Usually she had her secretary bring tea or coffee directly to her office, specifically to avoid going out there and making everyone nervous. But now she was making the trip to the tea room herself—except, of course, that the thermos was just a pretext, and when she reached the tea room she walked straight past it without going inside.

She quietly opened the main door to the department and stepped out into the corridor. A cleaner was there with her trolley, waiting for the lift to arrive. She glanced at Maria but made no attempt to greet her. Maria didn't recognize the cleaner and assumed this meant the cleaner wouldn't recognize her, either. She felt herself relax.

She let the cleaner enter the lift first, then shrank in after, keeping her eyes on the transparent plastic bottles filled with blue cleaning fluid in the trolley. When the lift was about halfway down it shuddered strangely, making the blue fluid slosh inside the bottles, and in that moment of weightlessness Maria cried out in alarm.

'We're too high up,' said the cleaner. The lift doors had not yet opened, and she spoke as though talking to herself.

'You're right, much too high up,' whispered Maria. She wished the cleaner would say something else, but for the rest of the journey down all she heard was the buzzing in her own ears.

11

When Maria suggested a couple of days at a temple retreat in the mountains, Professor Q did not object. The hike up there seemed a good way to test how well his body had recovered from his illness. Since returning from the auction he had been relieved, although at the same time a little disappointed, to find that Aliss's eyes had stopped following him around.

The temple Maria selected was one the hiking group had been to many times before, and they set off into the mountains as they always did: sun hats on and walking poles in hand, like a flock of determined pilgrims. They were not exactly quick, and in fact were frequently overtaken by younger hikers, but neither were they slow; they kept a steady pace. The mountain air was moist, carrying on it the tang of grass, and everybody was in good spirits. Well, everybody except Professor Q, who found the group's language strangely impenetrable, as though there were words within their words, and every time he looked up at the rays of sunlight piercing the tree canopy, he felt dizzy.

The path was narrow, shaded by trees on both sides. A flutter of yellow swallowtail butterflies drifted past, and the group exclaimed admiringly. Someone started to sing. Meanwhile, Professor Q was seeing things no one else could see. He had hiked the trail before, and knew the mountains well, but he barely recognized the scenery that now surrounded him. Walking between the smooth, straight, white-speckled tree trunks felt like walking through a forest of female legs. Something wet landed on his face. He wiped his cheek. Was it rain? No, not rain, but spray from a small waterfall; his companions were climbing over rocks to drink from its crystalline waters. He gazed at the cascading stream, hearing in its splashes the sweet, joyful cries of a woman.

It was cooler up there in the mountains. Breezes shook the leaves, and their rustling sounded full of whispers. The sky was darkening by the time the group arrived at the Temple of Bliss, where they were greeted by a monk wearing a pair of glasses and an expensive-looking watch. After they had made their (not insignificant) donations, they were led into a large hall. Some of them lit incense, and others knelt to shake tubes of fortune sticks. Professor Q stood to one side, as he usually did, only this time there was nothing cynical or bored about his expression. On the contrary, he was fascinated by the naked women carved into the temple pillars and beams. He had no recollection of seeing deities like these in Buddhist temples before. Their breasts were round and full, they had sashes tied around their waists, and their legs leapt elastically into the air; only their faces were undefined. This was when Aliss's eyes reappeared. Professor Q felt a jolt of pleasure, swiftly followed by panic that the monks would discover his secret. He glanced furtively around the hall.

A small monk approached and asked if he would like to come to the scriptorium. The monk looked like a little girl, although his robe was too loose to give much away about the body concealed beneath the fabric. Professor Q turned down the monk's offer, claiming he had plans to enjoy the garden instead. To give credence to this statement, he then walked outside to the pond, where he watched koi flashing through the water and felt his mouth fill with an unpleasant, fishy taste.

Later that evening the monks prepared dishes the group had ordered, setting down a centrepiece of taro sculpted into the shape of a fish. Maria picked off a piece for her distracted husband, but all he tasted was the nasty fishiness from earlier.

It had been a long day and everyone went to bed soon after dinner. The professor and three other husbands were assigned a dormitory furnished with two sets of bunk beds. Before long, the room filled with rumbling snores.

Professor Q lay awake in his top bunk, staring at the blank ceiling above. Suddenly, a tiny crack appeared in the plaster. The crack expanded, opening up to discharge a fist-sized plastic doll that hit him directly in the crotch. Before he could move away, several more dolls followed. With one hand over his mouth to muffle his cries, he used the other to untie his pyjama bottoms and check for damage to his penis. He found the dolls clustered around it, as if about to commence some kind of meeting. But rather than talk, they extended long, thick tongues (tongues much bigger than their bodies) and innocently, enthusiastically, like children with ice cream cones, they began to lick. They licked Professor Q's erection until the pleasure was excruciating, almost unbearable, and all he could do was give in to the sensation, now clamping both hands over his mouth.

He woke the next morning to find his sheets splattered with dried semen. While his roommates continued to sleep, he quietly remade the bed.

The sky was growing light when he arrived back in the main hall and, without really meaning to, he knelt before the dancing immortal carvings to pray. A monk came to stand beside him, palms pressed together in greeting.

'Sadhu! Sadhu!' said the monk, bringing his head to his hands. 'Well done, you.'

Professor Q looked up from his prayers and saw the monk's eyes glint green. The thought that the monk was also not originally from Nevers made him feel familiar somehow; closer.

'I beg you, Master, show me the way.'

'Days pass, life grows shorter. What joy is left for a fish in too little water?'

'Yes, days pass. But what do you mean? That it's too late to chase my dreams?'

The monk chuckled loudly and ran his hands over his head, pushing back his hood to reveal a shock of thick, golden curls. The professor's heart pounded: wasn't this the magician from the night of the auction?

'Days pass but another always comes. And who knows in which direction time will run?'

The magician reached into his robe and produced a pocket watch, its second hand ticking in a clockwise direction. Then he twisted a knob on the side, making the hand turn backwards, and the hall darkened.

'What time is it?' asked Professor Q.

The magician grinned.

'Ask, and it shall be given you; seek, and ye shall find; knock, and it shall be opened unto you; for every one that asketh, receiveth; and he that seeketh findeth; and to him that knocketh it shall be opened. Does it really matter what time it is? What matters is where you want to go!'

The magician flung open a hidden door, behind which stairs ascended steeply. Where would they lead our professor? The door swung shut behind him and all he could do was climb. Stairs. A corridor. Time seemed to have flipped upside down; it was all so familiar. At the top of the stairs, a skylight. Beyond the skylight, unobtainable sky. Tasteless, odourless, colourless sky, every last crack sealed tight, and then Professor Q was back on the antiques street once again.

It appeared to be long past midnight. The shops had their metal shutters pulled down, all of them grimy silver. The city had turned its back. Professor Q felt that time had become very thin, like one of those silent used-up cicadas, its discarded shell brittle and easily crushed. Aliss's shophouse was covered in scaffolding and green construction netting. Closed down, just like the magician had said. On the other side of it was a steep slope. A stream of luminous sewage gushed shamelessly along the gutter, before rearing like a serpent and slithering up the slope.

Professor Q had thought he knew those Valeria Island streets, but this strange new atmosphere made him realize he had never set foot in the area so late at night. He imagined all the people already asleep, headed into their dreams, following forks in paths invisible to them during the day. The city had expanded to several times its usual size. It was airier now, its substance transformed into a porous honeycomb; one misstep and he risked falling into one of its holes where he would no longer be able to distinguish space or time, and from which he would never re-emerge. But precisely because it was dangerous, it was also full of unknown potential.

He climbed the cracked slope and turned into a dark alley, where an acrid urine stench pierced his nostrils. Something was creaking. Messy piles of old wood and bamboo baskets were all over the ground, the spaces between them strewn with litter. Behind them, at the far end of the alley amid mounds of junk, was an enormous music box.

It was lying on its side, the lid facing Professor Q like a door, with a big copper key sticking out of it. He turned the key ninety degrees to the right, then another ninety degrees to the right, and the lid sprang open. Aliss wasn't lying down hugging her knees anymore: she was squatting in front of him, her knees spread wide. Her clothes were all gone, and he could see the delicate green veins around her nipples. The hair between her legs was freshly trimmed and within that hair was a slightly parted mouth. Aliss's body had so many mouths! This mouth, another mouth of partially visible teeth, and those two mouths inlaid with changing-colour eyeballs. Her palms were open and every mouth on her body was crying out to him, soundlessly: *Come here! Come here!* He walked joyfully into the box to join her, remembering to close the door as he went. Professor Q's body was fifty years old, the bones and blood vessels inside it all a little stiffer than they used to be, and now, just as this body could finally testify to the softness of romance, a dark world rose to engulf it.

12

There would be no point asking our blindsided protagonist how it all happened. The only thing Professor Q could tell you, his tone curiously detached, was that it felt as if a pack of wolves had come rampaging through his life. He firmly believed his old friend Owlish was secretly in charge, orchestrating everything, and all he could do was stand by and watch.

Four burly workmen dressed in repulsive, mustard-yellow overalls had showed up at his flat one morning, just after Maria left for work. He was still half-asleep and only faintly recalled going to answer the door, reacting to the diabolical noise of an insistently rung doorbell. Next thing he knew, the men had swept in, armed with rolls of packing tape and planks of wood. Before long, they were hauling sealed boxes out of the study, overalls straining with exertion, glinting buttons threatening to pop off. Professor Q sat on the living room sofa and watched as they packed up his decades-old collection of books, toys, scrolls, sculptures, and DVDs, filling box after box after box. It was hard to believe so much could ever have fitted inside his tiny study.

He was satisfied with the proceedings, less so with the workmen carrying them out. They seemed to be excessively large and bulky, and crashed through the building as though trying to alert everyone in the vicinity to their presence.

He went outside the flat and paced anxiously up and down the hallway. The boy next door stared at him from behind a security grille. He was crouched like a frog, gripping the metal bars with both hands, his expression oddly vacant. Professor Q tried to pretend nothing out of the ordinary was happening, which only made him more awkward. Eventually he gave up, retreating into his flat just as the workmen were struggling to heave out a large cupboard, apparently their final item.

He stood for a while in the living room, gazing through the study doorway to the emptied room beyond. A small patch of sunlight wavered on one of the grey walls, like a hand stroking a torso from which a tumour has recently been excised. He felt as though a hand were also stroking his torso, soothing his anxieties. He really did feel better: with all the junk gone the room seemed limp, its air thin and depleted, but underneath it all there was a pregnant feeling, a sense of new life about to begin.

What you need is a love nest. He recalled Owlish's words, nodding to himself in agreement.

A truck and then a fishing boat transported him and his belongings to an abandoned island. After all his years in Nevers, he was astonished to discover an island he hadn't known existed. The fishing boat anchored at a small beach, behind which a line of houses looked out to sea. The island must have seen better days because the houses were in ruins, clearly long uninhabited. Further back, on top of a hill, stood a small church. Its white walls were smothered in ivy, but there was still something pert and lovely about it, like a roosting pigeon. A minuscule cross sprouted from the join of the A-frame roof, suggesting it was the work of early Valerian missionaries. But who the hell would choose to come to a place like this now?

Someone like you, the professor heard Owlish respond, teasingly. *Someone with secrets to keep.*

The key slid into the keyhole like a reptile darting into its burrow.

Professor Q flicked his wrist and the lock clicked open. From the doorway, he could see to the back wall, and the wooden carving of Jesus Christ on the cross hanging there. As an atheist, he was not in the habit of visiting churches. The only time he went inside them was during holidays in Europe, on guided tours, when the extravagant domed ceilings covered in angels and saints always made his chest feel tight; if he happened to arrive during the hymns, all his hair stood on end. Why did Owlish have to choose a church, of all places?

Thankfully, this church had a more modest ceiling than its European counterparts, its wooden arches low enough that heaven still seemed far away. And, somehow, Owlish had already unpacked: the space was full of bookcases double the professor's height, his books lined up neatly along their shelves. The pews had been cleared out of the nave to make way for an enormous antique four-poster bed made of peach wood, with muslin drapes on all four sides. The rest of the space had been remodelled into a contemporary living room featuring a sofa, desk, refrigerator, bathroom facilities, and surround-sound system. The professor's Mephistopheles and Don Quixote artworks, along with other pieces previously shoved miserably out of sight, were now proudly displayed on the two carved wooden pulpits, each item protected by a gleaming glass case.

Then there was Aliss, her stage set up right beside the bed. She was dressed in a pristine white ballerina costume and posed like a swan, ready to welcome the church's new master.

Although the island seemed to be unpopulated, Professor Q was still pleased to see the main windows covered with thick, black curtains. There were also large paintings propped along the two side walls, including a triptych of the Garden of Eden, the mortal world, and Hell. Was this from his collection? If so, it couldn't have seen the light of day for years; he had completely forgotten about it. Adam and Eve were so young and nubile! What a pity God had chosen to come between them, and what a pity every bird and beast had to be confined to its own particular place. You could hardly call the Garden of Eden unoppressive. But the mortal world was different. How liberated those men and women seemed to be—their naked bodies piled on top of one another like fallen petals, their hands clasping clusters of grapes bigger than their faces or reaching for the forbidden fruit that dangled in abundance from surrounding branches. Some of them lay spread-eagled among fallen fruits, others among eggshells. They poked freshly cut flowers into each other's anuses, wrote musical scores on one another's backsides, played songs on bird-beak flutes. For Hell, which the professor had assumed would be even more interesting, the artist had chosen dark colours, which had only grown darker with age. Even when he got very close, Professor Q still couldn't make out the details.

He turned, noticing a dressing table with a three-way mirror. He went over to it and sat down. He had no interest in looking at his own ageing face; what he wanted was for the mirror to give him a clearer view of the church interior. But rather than making the room more visible, the mirror dragged everything out and chopped it up, creating a chain of overlapping images, making a two-dimensional world into something as grand and complex as a pipe organ. Perhaps the astonishing thing was not that he had lived so many years in Nevers without knowing that such an island, or such a church, existed, but rather that, in all the cities he had lived before, there had never been a place like this one—somewhere willing to accept him and all his treasures. Treasures he had been gathering like secrets, gorgeous, resplendent things, which were now in the mirror before him, replicated, larger than life. Aliss was there too, reborn many times over, watching him from inside all those parallel worlds. Her gaze no longer scared him. In fact, her eyes felt the way the sun does in dreams: encouraging, nourishing of everything that the dull, tasteless, real world chooses to forbid.

13

Professor Q rediscovered the joy of wrongdoing. Every day now he left his flat or his university office with the reptilian key in hand, stealing away to the secret world of the church and the music box. He liked to pick Aliss up and arrange her on a chair in front of the dressing table, then to stand behind her and brush her fine, soft hair with a genuine boar-bristle hairbrush, all the while scouring the mirror for glimpses of the secretive eyes concealed beneath her long lashes.

Aliss rarely wore her restrictive ballerina costume anymore. Every few days, Professor Q would dress her in something new— silk underwear, tiny hot pants, stockings and suspenders, a tuxedo, an evening gown, a cape—taking inspiration from his female students, young women he saw around Valeria Island, and models in fashion magazines.

As the weeks went by, he gained a better understanding of how Aliss and her music box functioned. The middle layer of the box was inlaid with glass, through which you could admire the teeth of a metal comb running over a metal roller; if you pulled out the bottom layer, it revealed itself as a cavernous drawer filled with seven spare rollers. All you had to do was switch over the roller above, wind it up, and the box would start playing a new tune. The top layer was the stage, and as soon as you clipped Aliss's feet into her ballet shoes she would dance across it to the music, a different dance for each tune. How the professor marvelled at the things her body could do. Such flexibility, and so many contortions; with each new piece of music, she seemed to become an entirely new woman.

Sometimes Professor Q would enjoy these performances from the sofa while sipping a glass of gin or whisky, interpreting Aliss's movements as coded messages from her body to his. Other times he experimented with her, laying her out in exotic new starting postures to see what would happen. He quickly came to know Aliss's anatomy as intimately as he did his own hands—the swell of her bottom, her pink fingernails with their ivory crescent tips, how far she could twist her knees, the way her hair took on different hues according to the light.

He didn't usually make her dance more than once a day, and afterwards he always carried out a careful inspection of her hands, arms, ankles, and knees. Temporarily abandoning his university research projects, he threw himself into learning how best to protect and maintain dolls and music boxes. Whenever his hands reached for the skittish nubs of Aliss's knees, he would think once again that, although he might be getting on in years, there was still time to prove himself an attentive lover.

For make no mistake: even after all that time cooped up in the church, Professor Q's love life was far from boring. Every day he and Aliss would spend a while sitting side by side in a custommade two-seater office chair. The chair was upholstered in an outlandish leopard-print fabric, and designed so that they could both be at the desk reading or writing at the same time. When he encountered a particularly exciting passage, or had a sudden brilliant idea, Professor Q would turn to Aliss and look at her a certain way (gently or intensely, depending on the occasion) and Aliss—beautiful, empathetic, darling Aliss!—would never fail to give him the same unspoken but nevertheless unwaveringly encouraging response. Her pouting rosebud lips were always so contented, so sure of themselves, and her glimmering eyes, their colour shifting like the sea, communicated to him the message: *Yes, I get it. I completely understand.*

As a lover, Professor Q was intellectually and emotionally beyond reproach. He pushed his imagination to the limits coming up with different ways for him and Aliss to connect. For example, one day, who knows how or where from, he appeared carrying a snow-white rocking horse with a flowing golden mane. A gentle nudge to the rocker, and it was off! With, of course, Professor Q and Aliss astride it, both of them entirely nude. The professor had his arms around Aliss's waist, and imagined himself a prince from a fairy tale. Not one of those sanitized, puritanical fairy tales written for children, but a folk tale full of lust and passion.

'You see? The moon smiles upon us!'

He pointed at one of the paintings, his mouth pressed to Aliss's ear.

'Next time, we can change the scenery. Snow, rolling countryside . . . even, if you prefer . . . the underworld.'

14

Professor Q could no longer keep to his schedule of being home before Maria every evening. Once upon a time he had been as obedient as Cinderella, but now, all too often, he stayed out well past midnight, tiptoeing home and sliding carefully into bed, hoping not to wake his sleeping wife. Sometimes he would clutch her arm or thigh in his sleep, dreaming he was locked in a passionate embrace with Aliss.

Now that he had his church hideaway, he was increasingly disinclined to return to Lone Boat University. The rare times he did venture onto campus, the world around him seemed to vanish into his blind spot.

Perhaps we can say that Aliss opened one of Professor Q's eyes and closed the other. Strolling through the university grounds, he didn't see the signs plastered all over the cafeteria walls and the noticeboards outside the library. Slogans full of exclamation points protested the groundless disqualification of an election candidate, the malicious destruction of the student newspaper offices, the school's decision to force students to take Northern language exams, police raids on student dormitories. The notices had been torn down and stuck back up again many times over, and now looked fragile and close to losing their respective battles.

Professor Q walked up the grassy slope to the statue of the university's founding father, wondering idly at the metal barricades around it. The statue looked just as sturdy as always. What threat could it possibly pose to passers-by? Little did he know, the university management was not worried about the statue posing a threat to others; they were worried about the crowds of students who had taken to gathering around it. The students had been coming with banners and signs and pasting slogans all over the old Confucian's robes in protest at the university's clampdown on student 'troublemakers'. The Confucian was a fitting ally, given his persecution at the hands of the Vanguard regime and subsequent flight to tiny little Nevers with his wife. The statue was not yet fully cleaned up but this made no difference to Professor Q: his eyesight newly impaired, he failed to notice any of the slogans at all.

Later that day he was giving a lecture, absent-mindedly clicking through slides on his computer, when a beam of sunlight broke through the window and sliced through his line of vision. The white walls around him transformed into flashing warning signs, alerting him to the fact that, in his one-hundred-capacity lecture hall, only three students remained.

He stopped talking and crossed his arms over his chest, surveying the hall with the detached, contented expression of someone enjoying a theatre production. The boy in the front row stopped chewing on his pen and looked up in confusion. The girl at the back of the hall kept scribbling notes for a while, then finally stopped and looked up too. Meanwhile the only other student in the room stayed slumped against a window, apparently fast asleep. With the professor's lapse into silence, the rumble of the sleeping student's snores seemed amplified.

It was a preposterous scene, and Professor Q's obvious amusement only seemed to unsettle the students further.

'Why aren't you out there doing something worthwhile?' he asked them. 'It's a lovely sunny day and here you are with your noses stuck in books of dead letters! Analysis and discourse are no way to get inside a poem, you have to start living! Go out there! Get in touch with the flesh and blood of the real world!'

He left his lectern and marched down the right side of the hall to the door, throwing it open and gesturing for the students to exit. They looked at one another in shock, unsure whether he was serious, then hurriedly gathered their belongings.

But there was one other student, one the professor had not noticed in his original count, who remained seated. In fact, it wasn't a student, but his or her shadow. It didn't make any sense, how could a shadow be sitting there unattached to a body? Lacking the courage to go over and ask, Professor Q returned to his lectern and barked, 'You! What are you still doing here?'

'Why would I leave?' replied the shadow. 'The real lesson has not yet begun.'

The professor was mystified. A shadow, speaking as loudly as a human? And what was this about a so-called real lesson? The hall lights slowly dimmed and the shadow became less distinct. The automatic power-saving system was kicking in. Professor Q hurried over to the shadow, but as he reached its empty seat he heard the loud bang of machinery coming to a halt, and it was as though the heart of the lecture hall had given out. In the ensuing darkness, everything in the room—including the shadow, including him—suddenly ceased to exist.

15

The love between Aliss and Professor Q existed outside the bounds of the common world. There was nothing transactional about it: in all that he did for Aliss, Professor Q asked for nothing in return. But you know how it goes. Whether you like it or not, a butterfly flaps its wings and unsettles the cosmos, one ocean wave births another ocean wave, a gust of wind builds, inevitably, into another gust of wind. Consider the ballerina doll, used to spending her days inside the dark, quiet confines of her music box, which the professor now opened up whenever he pleased, thrusting her into the realm of his wildest fantasies. Think of it from her perspective. Imagine the upheaval!

Day after day, Professor Q would press his lips to Aliss's earlobes, slide his fingers into her hidden crevices, and crawl like a clumsy reptile over the undulating topography of her body, leaving damp vestiges in his wake. In these moments of high passion, he would think, To hell with the Nevers mountain trails! Because this was true adventure. Here he had secret paths, wild abandon, the thrill of the unexpected. Here he was witness to an exciting new landscape Nevers had previously kept hidden from him, and it felt as if he were standing high on a mountain summit. He was afraid, yes, but not daunted; he was exhilarated by his fear, even found himself embracing his terror of death. Ah, Aliss! How he clung to her body, so worked up he didn't even know where to direct his death wish.

Aliss considered the professor's messy body an external disruption, but nothing he did with it was anywhere near as unsettling to her innermost being as his daily sessions playing music to her, reciting poetry to her, or sitting with her reading all those novels and philosophical tomes.

Professor Q, too, had been undergoing some transformations. Inside the church, his tongue became forked and he found himself able to say all kinds of new, unexpected words, words with meanings that glimmered like diamonds, full of endless potential. He began, as though possessed, to refute and expand on great philosophical and academic debates, seeking to express his views on love, time, consciousness, desire, existence, and as yet unnamed new fields of thought. Against the high church walls, his stocky frame appeared as a strapping silhouette. And of course all this only made him want Aliss more. Aliss, his arousing, uncritical, never-doubting audience of one. Never had his mind been so sharp! Never had his opinions been so incisive and thought-provoking! Sometimes he surprised even himself. He intensified his efforts to note down the contents of his impromptu speeches. The themes were still a little unclear, the logic perhaps a little shaky, but eventually those notes would be the basis for an important academic work (or a novel?), he felt sure of it. This was his ticket to greatness. Inside the church, he also began to write poetry again. After all, talent takes time to mature—who said it was too late to become a great poet?

One day, feeling inspiration strike, he kissed Aliss on the forehead, locked up the church, and set off on a walk around the island. He strolled along the beach for a while, then climbed another small hill. From the lookout spot, he realized he could see, atop the distant line of the Nevers mountain range, a familiar grey building.

Familiar, except the new perspective gave him pause—was it, could it really be, the same university office building where he usually went to work? That would mean Lone Boat was to the north-west of the island. He gazed for a while at the construction's expressionless façade. The daylight made the windows appear blacked out, and the wall colour seemed to grow increasingly dull and gloomy the longer he looked at it. What would anyone be doing stuck in the office on such a beautiful day?

The face of the newly hired Assistant Professor W came to mind. That poor W. Once so fresh, bursting with youth, but less than a year in the role and his skin was already sagging and obvious grey streaks had appeared in his jet-black hair. At recent faculty meetings, when there had been all that talk of high school recruitment drives, writing up department reports, and whatever other menial administrative tasks anyone could come up with—hadn't all those jobs been delegated to W? Yes, that was right, and his expression had revealed not a trace of annoyance. If anything, he had seemed grateful. Perhaps it would pay off and he would get his promotion, but if even the secretaries were offloading work onto him, what hope was there?

The less he went in to the university, the better Professor Q felt. His mind was clearer, and he felt ten years younger. He narrowed his eyes and extended his right thumb, trying to blot out the distant office building. He imagined knocking the whole thing down with one quick push and chuckled to himself at the idea. Then he felt a flash of unease and hurriedly scanned his surroundings. The narrow path up the hill was lined with tall trees, which cast slanting shadows across the ground. There was no one there. Of course there wasn't; the island was uninhabited. He was worrying about nothing. He turned back to face the university and thought of himself sitting behind one of those windows, day in, day out, working like an automaton, and suddenly felt absolutely furious.

'I've given that place my youth! Look at those windows. Behind every one, a sweaty, overworked professor, buried in funding applications, university promotion plans, just piles and piles of paperwork . . .'

Professor Q muttered under his breath, squinting at the building, and once again extended his mighty thumb to block the whole thing out. Standing there on the island, he felt like a new man. Never again he would he let anyone walk all over him. From now on, no one would tell him what to do! Once again, he chuckled at the idea.

Aliss's transformations were quieter than the professor's, and slower to take effect. From his perspective, she was the same as always: mute, pretty, mysterious, with those eyes that closed when she lay down but otherwise remained as wide open as the universe, fearlessly absorbing the world before them, framed by lashes like fluttering wings. But this was all a prelude to the mutation of a life form—it was just that nobody knew the exact moment this mutation would take place.

It was dark by the time Professor Q returned to the church. In recent weeks, every nightfall had made him melancholy. He straightened out Aliss's clothes and took the boar-bristle brush to her hair, carefully rectifying the mess he had made of it earlier. Reflected in the three-way mirror, Aliss looked like the Holy Trinity, like a God so far removed from Professor Q's existence that he might as well have dreamt her up. She would never truly be able to join him in his earthly pleasures.

Before leaving the church, he always locked Aliss back inside the music box, following what had become an extensive, almost ceremonial process. He would oh-so-softly inspect every inch of her neck, or stroke each one of her toes, before reluctantly placing her inside the box. Then, just like her former master, he would give the key two ninety-degree turns to the left, trapping her in the dark world within.

Today, however, his final inspection was interrupted by something shaking in his trouser pocket. He reached inside and realized it was his phone, vibrating with a message alert. Maria had written to remind him it was their tenth wedding anniversary. He had nothing planned. He completed his box-closing ritual in a distracted haze, turning the key ninety degrees to the left, then ninety degrees back to the right. In his haste, he failed to notice that his desk lamp was still on, or that one of the windows was still open behind its black-out curtain. No sooner had he closed the church doors than the impatient wind that had been brewing all day could hold back no longer, and it crawled on in.

The wind crawled across the floor, across the desk, over the scribbled-in notebooks, and then it started to walk, then to run, as if touched by the Holy Spirit. On the desk, pages rustled against one another, speaking in barely audible whispers. The walls were ripe and shuddering. The object locked in the darkness was half asleep, half waiting to wake up. Creaking hesitantly, the heavy door of the antique music box was being pushed open from the inside.

16

And off went Professor Q, part-time master of the church! Having left his overgrown little island and returned to Lion Slope, he hunched forward, his footsteps quickened, and he transformed back into a dutiful husband, a frustrated academic, a man in late middle age perspiring heavily in his rush to be on time for a date.

Maria had booked a table at a well-run chain restaurant serving Western-style food, not far from their flat. It was one of the places they ate at from time to time, on days Maria didn't feel like cooking. On this particular night, even from some distance away, the restaurant seemed different from usual. Was it the droplet-shaped fairy lights strung around the black glass walls? Many businesses had put up special decorations to mark the tenth anniversary of Nevers's 'return' to the motherland, hoping to attract tourists who had come over for the celebrations. Maybe that had been the restaurant's motivation. But maybe it wasn't the lights that made Professor Q sense something was different; maybe it was the white roses. He was carrying a bunch in such full bloom they were on the verge of collapse, their heady scent almost convincing him that he really was on his way to a romantic rendezvous.

In all their years of marriage, he and Maria had never once celebrated their wedding anniversary, and he was a little baffled at this sudden display of interest. His puzzlement only grew when he entered the restaurant and saw Maria waiting for him at their table, also looking different from usual. She came into sharper focus as he approached, and he saw that she had shiny red grease smeared over her lips, pink powder dabbed across her cheeks, and, around her neck, a pearl necklace he had given her many years before.

He handed her the bouquet, wondering how he was going to explain being half an hour late. To his surprise, Maria seemed unbothered by the time and simply smiled appreciatively at the flowers.

He exhaled quietly and sat down.

'I almost didn't recognize you,' he said, regretting the words as soon as they were out of his mouth. He meant it as a compliment but the tone was all wrong; it sounded like he was mocking her.

'I could say the same for you,' said Maria, looking straight into his eyes. His stomach lurched. Maria's face was so soft and welcoming, yet her words felt like an attack.

She was sitting in front of a dark glass wall. He shifted incrementally on his chair until he could see his own reflection behind her. He hadn't had a haircut in months, and his curls were getting long. He was wearing a short-sleeved shirt with a jaunty silk cravat, an outfit he had picked out carefully before leaving home that morning. The thought now struck him that he looked like a has-been country singer.

Maria said nothing further and signalled to the waiter. After they had each ordered their individual meal sets, Maria asked for a bottle of red wine.

This was extremely out of character. Professor Q stared at his wife. She was getting on in years, but took such good care of her skin that her face was as full and unlined as a pearl. Her health was robust, her career smooth and successful, her life exactly as it should be; she suffered neither on account of work nor on account of carnal cravings, which was really quite the achievement. He felt a surge of jealousy and leaned back in his chair, allowing the feeling to wash over him. Even without checking his reflection he could feel how his tired flesh drooped. A professor seemed like a respectable enough job, but in truth he was a nobody in university terms, trampled over by anyone who pleased. And then there were his years and years of struggles to contain his desires—what was he, some kind of tragic clown?

The waiter poured the wine, and Professor Q and Maria clinked glasses.

'To marriage!' said Maria.

'To marriage!' said Professor Q, unable to tell whether Maria was being sarcastic.

'Talking of which, you haven't come hiking for a while.'

'Work's just been so busy lately.' To add credibility to his statement, he furrowed his brow.

'Really? I thought all the students were on strike?'

Professor Q's hand started to shake, setting off a series of tiny waves inside his glass. On strike? Was that why nobody was showing up to his lectures? He forced a laugh, to counteract the tremor.

'Oh, it's precisely because of the strike that we're so busy. Almost every day there's another meeting to discuss what to do about it.'

'It must be such a headache. What has the university decided?'

Professor Q was confused. If the students were really on strike, why hadn't he received a single email about it from the university management? Admittedly, he had not been paying close attention to the news of late, but even so it seemed improbable that he wouldn't have heard anything. Senior management must have held a closed-door meeting to discuss their plan of action, and left him out because he was too junior. That must have been it.

But then he recalled an encounter with Professor W in a university corridor a few weeks earlier. At first, W didn't seem to notice him; in fact, he walked right past him, as though circumventing an anonymous obstacle in his path. When Professor Q called out,

W turned briefly and said he was rushing to catch a meeting. In retrospect, there had been something strange about his manner—a smugness, an underlying awkwardness. At the time, Professor Q had been mildly offended by the rebuff but hadn't given much thought to exactly what meeting W was racing off to. Now it struck him that they were in the same department, so how could there have been a meeting he knew nothing about? Had W been heading to a discussion about how to handle the student strike?

Then again, did it really matter? Professor Q had no grand aspirations to be at the centre of power, and even less desire to get involved in politics. What he cared about was securing tenure, and he was almost ready to submit his application for the third time. Just the other day, the department chair had slapped him on the back and told him, chummily, that this time he would make it. *I've seen your performance evaluations and you should have no trouble at all!* Clearly, he was at a critical juncture: he had to be especially careful, couldn't afford to let any flies into the ointment.

'If it's confidential, you don't have to tell me,' said Maria, in the face of his prolonged silence. 'I work in government, I know how these things are.'

She paused, then continued: 'But how about this weekend we go on a picnic? Not with the group, just us. Just you and me.'

Professor Q looked down at his plate and twirled a large clump of spaghetti around his fork, then crammed it into his mouth. All he could think about was Aliss, standing on her stage ready to dance.

'You know,' added Maria, 'this landscape won't be here forever. It could all be gone tomorrow.'

Professor Q wasn't sure what she meant by this last comment, but eventually he nodded, and they clinked glasses once again.

And so it was that Professor Q spent the following two days out with his wife. They walked up into the Nevers mountains and along the

Nevers coast. They even rented a little boat and went rowing on a lake. Without either of them saying anything aloud, they each knew the other was flooded with memories of their university courtship. At bedtime, Maria silently removed her clothes and reached for Professor Q's hand. For Professor Q, caressing his wife's body felt like composing an academic article; he had to solemnly weigh each word. His hand travelled over her thighs, her waist, her breasts, her neck, and then he leaned over and kissed her: his article's concluding full stop.

Maria's breathing deepened and before long she was sleeping serenely against his chest. She looked like an angel. (He had never seen an angel, but if they did exist, what else could they possibly look like?) Even if she felt no desire for him, touching a female body like that had got him worked up, and he struggled to fall asleep.

He thought of Aliss, of that ballerina body he could arrange however he desired. He imagined her kneeling naked in the church, palms together, face towards the Jesus hanging over the altar, bottom thrust in the air. *Come on, Professor! Fuck me!* He could almost hear her pleading. But wait, it wasn't Aliss who was kneeling; it was him. A dark portal seemed to yawn open before him, hopeful as a lucky dip. He reached in and a hand came to meet his, yanking him inside. Professor Q knelt naked on the ground, bottom thrust in the air. It was silent in the church. No one was coming to fuck him. He continued to kneel, thinking desperately that no one was willing, no one would say *I do*—not even Jesus, the most loving, the most merciful.

17

It started to drizzle and never seemed to stop.

Spring in Nevers was quiet but brazen. It forced its way through walls, invading each and every household. Trails of green and white mildew grew to engulf wooden chairs and table legs, clambering into wardrobes and infesting leather overcoats that lurked at the back. Lurid yellow mushrooms sprouted from bus seats. Silent life forms burst forth in all kinds of new shapes and colours, and those trapped inside the church were no exception.

Let's rewind a little, to the evening Professor Q last left the church. As the door closed behind him, the lid of the antique music box began to creak open, pushed from the inside. Aliss's hands reached through the ensuing gap, her luminous white, barely parted fingers flexing like worms awakening from hibernation. Then came her glassy, colour-changing eyes, reopening as she became upright, slowly bringing the world around her into focus.

The church was dim, the only light coming from Professor Q's neglected desk lamp, which illuminated the desk and the book that lay open on top of it. The white rocking horse and the painting Aliss had seen while riding it were both submerged in shadow. Aliss still had a vague memory of the painting; she could conjure the scene. She crept out of the music box on all fours, like a cat (although highly skilled as a ballerina doll, she still needed some time to adjust to walking). She climbed shakily onto the two-seater desk chair and shifted around in search of a comfortable position, discovering that her spine fitted perfectly into the moulded back of the chair. She looked to her right and saw the presence that usually occupied the space beside her was gone. It didn't matter: she knew how to use her tiny fingers with their minuscule fingernails to turn the book's pages herself.

In the yellow glow of the lamp, Aliss stroked the pages, enjoying the sensation of lamp-warmed words and paper against her palms. Gradually, however, she began to feel unnerved by the shadows drifting around her. After some groping about, she located a switch that turned on all the other lights in the church.

The first thing she saw, inside the opened music box, was a small, leather-bound book with the handwritten title: *User Manual*. It was full of diagrams with handwritten captions, explaining the many positions a user could expect from their ballerina doll.

Aliss was not particularly interested, and began to explore the rest of the church. There were bookcases everywhere crammed with books; she remembered reading some of them with the man who was always coming to visit. They hadn't made much sense to her at the time, but they were certainly more fun than the user manual.

She followed a bookshelf until she reached the three-way mirror, where she sat down and saw her own face not once, but three times. Three times, but not at the same time; she had to choose. Whenever she turned, something vanished. She tried to touch these Alisses inside the mirror but her fingers hit against an ice-cold surface, leaving behind smeary prints. There was something there, in between the two worlds, blocking her from her other selves. She touched her cheek and the Alisses in the mirror did too. Her cheek was soft. Soft and not ice-cold, but not exactly warm either.

She stood up, attracted now by the sight of a large cupboard. The key had been left sticking out of the keyhole and it turned easily, with a click. Aliss started at the noise, dropping the key. She gazed at it for a while, lying there motionless on the ground, then she collected herself and eased open the door. The cupboard was packed with boxes and messy piles of strange-looking objects, but her attention went immediately to a shelf of neatly lined-up dolls.

They seemed to be a similar species to her, although one of them was without a body, and another had eyelids but no eyelashes. Their skin colour ranged from pale and glossy to dark and matte, and they were all looking straight at her with their different coloured eyes. The one with just a head had cascading golden hair, and a face that looked so delicate, so soft, that Aliss couldn't resist, she had to reach out and touch it. But it turned out to be hard and rough.

Then she noticed the Dolligal. The Dolligal was in an upright position, her arms reaching out as though cradling a moon, her legs bent outwards into a beautiful diamond. She was tiny, much smaller than Aliss, but her silver outfit looked like one Aliss used to wear; the cut of the bodice and the way the tutu fanned around her waist were almost identical. So were the shoes: sleek, glistening, tied up with ribbons criss-crossed around the ankle.

Aliss placed the Dolligal in her palm, holding her steady with her other hand, and carried her to the three-way mirror where she laid her down on the dressing table. The Dolligal's eyes closed. Aliss straightened out her arms, then her legs, arranging the Dolligal on the dressing table just like the man who was always coming to the church arranged her on the bed. Then it occurred to her that the Dolligal must be uncomfortable in such a restrictive outfit, and she began to undress her, first removing the ballet shoes, then the ballet costume, revealing the smooth body beneath. She traced its contours with a finger, drawing a line from the Dolligal's lips to her breasts to her stomach, then down to the place below.

She picked the Dolligal up again and watched her round blue eyes spring open, noticing something glimmer inside them. She poked one, gently at first, then much harder, until the eyeball sank. Bringing her eye to the empty socket, she saw that the dark space inside the Dolligal's head was empty too. Where had the eyeball gone? She shook the Dolligal and heard something knocking around inside her body.

She put the Dolligal down and turned back to the mirror, hoping to look properly at her own eyes, but whenever she moved their colour started to change. She opened her mouth and the mirror showed her a gaping black hole. What could such a hole be hiding?

Aliss stood up. She could see from her reflection that all she had on was a flimsy silk negligée. One tug on the shoulder straps and it slid to the floor. Now her breasts were in the mirror. She cupped them in her hands and they lay there like two living beings, snuggled into her palms. They weren't like the Dolligal's at all! These weren't smooth, perfectly circular mounds, but rather two faces; two little faces with only mouths. The mouths were round and slightly sticking out, and when she touched them she noticed tiny bumps around the edges. Feeling a sudden, electric thrill, she looked away from the mirror and stared down at her chest—what were they? Perhaps push buttons, or some kind of special mechanism?

She wanted to see herself more clearly, and remembered that the man had a wardrobe full of clothes to dress her in—yes, there it was. And, just as she had thought, when she walked over and opened it there was a full-length mirror stuck to the back of the door. Now she could see her lower body too: waist, belly, legs. Between her legs, there was a crop of hair. She sat down slowly, spreading her thighs, and there in between them was another face—another face with only a mouth, which had been closed but was now opening towards her, revealing a hole even deeper than the others. She shifted closer to the mirror, staring intently at the mouth, as though by doing so she would be able to hear it and all the secrets it was trying to tell her.

18

Out at sea, fog obscured the horizon. Professor Q sat aboard the boat headed for his island, wondering whether any of it really existed. Was there an island? Or a church? Only two days had passed since his last visit, but it felt like a lifetime. He couldn't remember what Aliss looked like. Instead, the sound of waves knocking against the boat was pulling him back to more distant memories. Thinking of his time in the box in the ship's hold, he hugged his knees to his chest, worried that long-ago transformation spell was regaining its effect. It was only when the boat captain tapped on his shoulder that he noticed the island and realized they had arrived. He disembarked and walked distractedly across the beach, then up the steps to the church. As he drew closer, he noticed someone in a fisherman's hat by one of the windows, apparently trying to see inside. He sped up, but the person ducked around the side of the building and vanished.

From outside the church, Professor Q saw that all the black-out curtains had been torn down. The squat little windows were thick, and slightly opaque, but they still offered a certain view of the situation inside: the room was now dazzlingly illuminated, clothes were strewn all over the floor, and there, sitting among them, was Aliss.

Professor Q raced in. Before he knew what was happening, Aliss had launched herself at him, pinning him to the floor. She was extraordinarily strong. Next, she gripped him by the ankles and held him aloft, letting him dangle like that for a while, staring in terror at the upside-down church. Then he was back on the floor, face up, and saw Aliss with her legs apart, readying to straddle his body like a horse. He managed to get up and stumble his way to the front of the church, to the sanctuary, the holy place, where he climbed onto the altar. Aliss was chasing after him, getting closer, until he yelled at her and she froze.

'Dressing table! Now!' he shouted, pointing towards the three-way mirror.

When Aliss didn't respond, he tried again. This time, whether because she'd understood or because she was acting on some plan of her own, she headed for the dressing table. She was an elegant dancer, but her gait was slow and clumsy. When she finally made it to the table and sat down, the professor heaved a sigh of relief. Was his doll malfunctioning? Or had he inadvertently pressed something and uncovered a hitherto unknown feature? (Little did he know, Aliss had been studying his *Kama Sutra*, learning new and exciting positions. He was woefully unprepared to become her test subject.)

Still watching Aliss, Professor Q eased himself down from the altar and sat on the floor. He looked more closely at the state of his church. It was a mess, and not just from the clothes—toys and books had been pulled off their shelves and thrown all over the floor, or left piled up on his desk. Could the doll really have done all this?

Aliss seemed about to stand up again and he started to panic, started to climb back on the altar, but all she did was walk over to the desk and sit down on their two-seater desk chair. She sat there quietly, her slender fingers leafing through an enormous book. Was it one of the atlases? Her face was pressed right up against the pages, as though she was profoundly short-sighted.

Curious, Professor Q crept up behind her. She was looking at a coffee-table book of Nevers landscape photography. The current photo was rows of tiny plastic bags, each one transparent and full to bursting with its own little sea, inside of which goggle-eyed gold-fish stared out at the camera. Aliss turned the page, arriving at an image of giant spinning tea cups, one containing a man and woman with their cheeks pressed together and their arms raised, making V shapes in the air. They too were looking directly at the camera, eyes squinted into four little cracks. Aliss rubbed a finger over their faces. Professor Q moved closer, pressing against her from behind. She turned, glancing at him briefly before something else caught her attention.

Sunlight was pouring in through a stained-glass window over the church doors, beaming patches of colour onto the floor. Aliss walked into the middle of them and threw her hands up, letting the coloured light flow between her fingers. She tilted her head up so that it landed on her forehead, nose, cheeks. She closed her eyes. A smile seemed to be appearing on her face. Then two breathy, shaky words of Valerian emerged from her lips: 'I . . . like . . .'

Professor Q could hardly believe his ears. The doll could talk! And in Valerian—was that where she was from? Valeria?

'I . . . like . . .' repeated Aliss. 'I like . . . light.'

She pointed to the big open flower depicted in the stained glass. Professor Q stared speechlessly at this doll—no, this beautiful crea-ture, this *woman*. His fear had receded; now he simply had no idea how to react. Aliss looked at him, then pointed to the photography collection on the desk.

'I . . . like,' she said again, pointing back to the window.

And this time he understood: Aliss was saying she wanted to go out.

He sat down at the desk, at a loss for words.

'Isn't this what you've been dreaming of all these years? The chance to fall in love with a real woman?'

It was Owlish talking, he was sure of it. And, here, at last, was such a woman. How could it be anything other than a sign from above?

'Ask, and it shall be given you; seek, and ye shall find; knock, and it shall be opened unto you.'

He raised his hands in surrender.

'Listen,' he said, softening his voice. 'I have to think. Just let me think.'

He got up from his chair and began pacing around the church.

Parading through the Nevers streets with this captivating young woman on his arm would be a dream come true. It was everything he had ever wanted. But he had a wife, he couldn't just go around frolicking with someone else—what if they ran into one of Maria's friends, or, God forbid, Maria herself? Not to mention his neighbours, his colleagues, his students . . . Aliss didn't understand, there were eyes everywhere!

'This could be your last chance for adventure,' said Owlish.

'Aliss—' said Professor Q, hesitantly. 'May I call you that?'

He waited, but she didn't reply.

'Listen. I'll think of something, I promise. But if we go out, you have to be quiet, keep your mouth shut, get back in your box—if you can do that, I'll take you to see the city. And, when the time's right, I'll let you out to walk around. Don't worry, I'll find a way.'

It was unclear whether she was satisfied with this proposal. She was silent, staring at him as though he were some kind of exotic life form, her gaze piercing his heart like tiny shards of glass. He started shivering again. A woman! He had really found himself a woman.

Blood rose in his face. He set about picking up the torn-down curtains, then fetched a ladder to rehang them.

'We have to get this done first,' he said to Aliss, while he worked. 'Some things are not for other people to see.'

Poor, clumsy Professor Q! It took a lot of effort, but eventually the church interior was once again shielded from view.

He blushed for a second time as he took off his clothes and climbed onto the four-poster bed, burrowing under the covers.

'How about . . . I mean, why . . . why don't you come in here?' he said to Aliss.

She was looking at the floor now, at the way her shadow fell across it, and she appeared deep in thought.

'You say . . . my . . . name . . . is . . . Aliss?'

He nodded.

'As far as I know, your only name. What's wrong, don't you like it?'

Aliss shook her head.

'I . . . don't know. I . . . don't know where it comes . . . from, or . . . what . . . it means.'

She paused.

'And you? Can . . . you . . . tell me . . . your . . . name?'

'Owlish,' blurted out Professor Q. 'In here, my name is Owlish.'

'Owl . . . ish,' repeated Aliss. 'Like . . . an owl?'

'Yes, something like an owl but also not like an owl. How can I put this? Do you know about amphibians? Creatures that are somewhere in between aquatic and terrestrial—from an evolutionary perspective, a kind of transitional species. If an owl is a bird with a head like a cat, perhaps we should say Owlish is a cat with a head like a bird? To be Owlish is to be a creature somewhere in between a mammal and a bird. To be Owlish is to be a bird that can't fly, at least not at the moment, but who can climb tall trees and pretend to be a bird, borrowing its nest from other birds. For now, that's what it must do to survive. But who knows what will happen next? Everything is changing.'

The explanation, seeming to arrive all in one breath, surprised even Professor Q. He couldn't wait any longer.

'Aliss,' he said, almost pleading with her. 'Aliss, come on, please come here. We'll take it slow. I'll be gentle.'

'Slow. Gentle,' said Aliss, and she seemed to understand: she crept across the church like a thief and then leapt onto the bed, nimble as a cat.

'Come in,' whispered the professor. 'Come under the covers with me. Get into bed.'

His voice was so soft. Aliss lowered hers too, repeating *slow, gentle, slow, gentle* as she slid into the bed beside him.

'Slow. Gentle,' recited Professor Q. He was already naked and now, with shaking hands, he reached out to undo Aliss's clothes.

Everything's going to be okay.

Ask, and it shall be given you.

Seek, and ye shall find.

Knock, and it shall be opened unto you.

For every one that asketh, receiveth; and he that seeketh findeth; and to him that knocketh it shall be opened.

Alas, poor Professor Q! The holy doors had been flung open but, when the time came for him to walk through, he wavered; he couldn't cross the threshold. After being hidden away for so long, after so many years left idle, his manhood, his most sacred tool, simply could not go through with it. At the most critical moment, it shrank and shied away.

Fuck.

19

At half a century old, all Professor Q wanted was a love affair, a proper love affair, for once in his life. Now that he finally had the chance to put his desires into action, nothing should have been left standing in his way. But things had been happening in Nevers, among them one small, seemingly insignificant thing that would nevertheless have grave consequences for our professor. And those of us here on the sidelines can only sigh, knowing it was precisely because of how completely he abandoned himself to romance that he remained so oblivious to the danger staring him in the face.

It was a day like any other in the city. Dusk was closing in, and every street in Lion Slope was thronged with vehicles enthusiastically spewing exhaust. Sales representatives dressed as animals and space aliens crowded the pavements, flooding the streets with marketing giveaways, making the air thick with flyers, and the scene repeated over and over again to infinity in the reflective building façades. The city at least gave the appearance of being joyful. Meanwhile, inside offices, shopping malls, and buses, powerful air conditioning reduced people to shivering wrecks. You could hear it in the unconscious dancing of their fingers, tapping against desks, keyboards, bus horns.

At half past six, a rousing song broke through the frenzy, cruising into people's turbulent thoughts like a tanker ploughing through waves. It was the national anthem of the Vanguard Republic, broadcast on all the television channels ahead of the evening news—one of the many new quirks to have come with the regime handover. The lyrics of the song described the Vanguard Party leading its people in a brave struggle to vanquish their enemy. Unfortunately, in a city like Nevers, the enemy was hard to identify. At pedestrian crossings, little men flashed green; on the sides of buildings, enormous female celebrities peered down from breast enhancement advertisements, blowing kisses with both hands. In one of the local cafeterias, Nevers residents awaited beef curry rice and condensed milk toast. As the song crashed in, they shrugged, laughed hollowly, let toothpicks fall into the remains of their soup.

On the cafeteria television, the only Southern-language channel in Nevers began playing the news. The reporters were all the same, all demure young women in pink suits and pussy-bow blouses; their lipstick was as carefully applied as their expressions, allowing only the most carefully considered of words to make it past their lips. The lead story had been the same for days, a mid-level scandal with which the diners were by now more than familiar. The screen filled once again with footage of the Lone Boat University library. Suited Ksanese VIPs entered through a revolving glass door, then slowly ascended a wide, red-carpeted staircase. The camera panned over the staircase walls, on which portraits of university presidents were arranged in chronological order all the way to the top. The portraits were almost identical, each one showing the gleaming painted face of yet another middle-aged man, but Lone Boat's current president was on camera gesticulating at them exuberantly, apparently introducing each former president to his esteemed guests. Then the group reached the top step and their expressions suddenly darkened: in the last frame, beneath a plaque bearing the current president's name, instead of the expected likeness they found (to use the newspaper parlance) 'a painting of an explicit nature'.

This time, the painting was only on screen for a fraction of a second. The footage had been cut down from its original length, rapidly giving way to a pretty news anchor reporting on the police response to the issue. The diners hissed in disapproval at the cut, although in reality the image was readily available to anyone with an internet connection. A few diners started up a discussion, claiming it was an exaggeration to call the painting explicit. It was just a picture of a man and woman who happened to be naked—in fact, only the man was naked, an odd-looking short guy, standing next to the silhouette of a ballerina. And their genders were not actually that easy to determine. If you looked closely enough, the man seemed to be in possession of a tiny penis, but his chest was strangely voluptuous, and the ballerina seemed to be female, but a long, tubular thing extended from between her legs.

In any case, a (not particularly valuable) portrait of a university president had been switched with this painting, which, in the great scheme of things, was a relatively innocuous prank. The reason this prank was making headlines all over the city was because it had coincided with the tenth anniversary of the Nevers handover, in honour of which Ksanese dignitaries, including the nation's premier, had been in the territory on an official visit. In anticipation of the celebration, Nevers police had taken a number of measures to ensure public security. Politically sensitive elements were arrested in advance; demonstrations were banned; splinter protests were immediately stifled, or blockaded far from the eyes of the visiting Ksanese officials. When the day came, the Vanguard Republic flag flew high, technicolour fireworks lit up the sky over Valeria Harbour, and prearranged crowds obediently braved the summer heat to line the streets in welcome. Everything went perfectly according to plan. Another bright spot in the official itinerary came in the aftermath of a spectacular fighter jet performance, when the premier put down his binoculars, banged the railing before him three times, and spoke three profoundly meaningful words, which would go on to spark intense debate among current affairs commentators: *Good . . . good . . . good!* The newly appointed police commissioner wiped his brow in relief. At long last, his mission was almost accomplished! The most important dignitaries soon accompanied the premier on a flight back home, and the commissioner saw no further reason to worry.

The next day, on the occasion of the Lone Boat library tour, library access was suspended and police made sure that the angry students—the ones with the bandanas and the slogan-spewing mouths—had been herded off campus ahead of time. The library doors and windows showed no signs of having been forced and, all in all, there was simply no way any student could have entered the main campus library on the day in question; the painting switch must have taken place earlier, when the library had been open as usual, the perpetrator presumably making use of a moment when the staff were distracted. But they hadn't chosen the fastest or most convenient of methods: rather than simply replacing the whole painting, they had removed the original portrait from its mount and inserted the new one into the frame in its place, resealing the back with sticky tape. It was hard to imagine such a time-consuming endeavour not attracting attention, or that, from the moment of the switch until the official tour, not a single person had noticed the difference. The consensus among the Nevers populace was that the university president was so widely disliked that the library staff, users, and security guards had all turned a blind eye to any suspicious behaviour.

Regardless, at the ensuing press conference, where the air conditioning was so forceful that microphones trembled in the shivering hands of participating journalists, the police commissioner was the only attendee who appeared to be sweating. It had not been simply a politically motivated act, he insisted to the crowd. No, it had been a deliberate challenge to police authority. As such, in order to uphold the honour of Nevers law enforcement, there would be no holds barred in getting to the bottom of the matter.

The case was still pending investigation, but the mainstream media (as the official government mouthpiece) wasted no time in linking it to the student protests of recent years, launching attacks on the behaviour of the opposition party and university students. This did nothing to prevent spoofs of the painting spreading like wildfire around the internet. The president's head was pasted in, next to the heads of various important political and business figures, and rumours began to resurface about under-the-table deals between the Lone Boat University management and the government, or the business-world elite. A little more innocent, perhaps, was the version featuring the Ksanese official's wife who had fainted during the library tour. In an animated rendering, the ballerina silhouette was given a loved-up version of the wife's face making come-hither eyes at the university president—leading some internet users to state with absolute certainty that the president and the official's wife were long-standing fuck buddies, their carnal union the physical embodiment of Nevers's undying love for the motherland, a promotion of profound, penetrating exchange between the two territories. All kinds of dark stories about the wife were subsequently unearthed, to the point that she declared she would never again set so much as a toe in the godforsaken, barbarous little territory, not for as long as she lived.

As for the explicit painting itself, for a brief moment it was an object of widespread fascination. A number of people were intensely curious about who had painted it. They declared it technically brilliant, the style reminiscent of Dalí. At a certain point, an anonymous Northern millionaire was reported to have secretly bought it, a claim which forced the Nevers police to put it on public display, despite its 'explicit nature', to prove that the evidence remained in their custody. Even so, they were making no headway on the case

125

whatsoever. The university had commissioned a new portrait of the president, although unfortunately there remained a while to go until its expected completion. In the meantime, they had removed the entire frame from the top of the library staircase. It had been hanging there for so long that the patch of grey wall beneath it was noticeably lighter than the rest of the wall around it, creating an intriguing, window-like effect.

What a shame Professor Q was too wrapped up in his romance to visit the university library! Had he gone, even if he failed to notice the newly blank space on the staircase wall, he might have at least overheard students or library personnel choking back laughter as they passed it by.

20

Professor Q was having the time of his life, his body positively bulging in its effort to contain his delight. True to his word, he found a way to take Aliss out and about in Nevers. It was yet another thing for which he had Owlish to thank, seeing as it was Owlish who provided the minivan. And it was no ordinary minivan: inside, behind the driver's compartment, it had been decked out with a wraparound sofa and sunken light fixtures in the ceiling. It had a record player, television, and minibar, and the windows were tinted, allowing passengers to see out but nobody to see in.

From inside this dreamy little world, Professor Q found himself falling back in love with the city he lived in, its garish shopfronts now seeming like gifts he could offer Aliss. With Aliss, too, he found himself falling in love in a whole new way. The girl in the van with him was someone new, reformed, and he didn't dare approach her in the same frenzied, careless manner as he had before. Now he behaved like a gentleman, staying decorously in his own seat, making polite, intellectual conversation. He asked her whether she remembered any of the books they had read together. At first her replies were disjointed and unilluminating, but she quickly gained fluency, stunning him with her insights. On some topics, she managed to revolutionize his thinking entirely. And when they talked about his collection of erotic works, she turned out to be much bolder than he was.

The pair of lovebirds chatted about everything under the sun while taking in all that Nevers had to offer. In the city centre, they passed brand-new, shimmering glass skyscrapers and the oldest of the crumbling, colonial-era buildings. Every so often, to give Aliss a clearer glimpse of a shop display, or a statue in a park, the van would slow, causing a long queue of honking cars to form behind it. Aliss would climb to the back of the van and look in fascination at the infuriated drivers, while the professor chuckled into his wine glass. Inside the minivan, Professor Q felt he was finally free. To hell with his university superiors! To hell with his wife and her old, lowbrow friends! Fuck them all! When the van reached unpopulated parts of the city, he would signal to the driver to stop. He and Aliss would get out and stroll blissfully along empty mountain trails, entering temples to watch incense sticks burn down to stubs, or sitting on stone benches to watch fish dart about in streams. Once, they even took a private helicopter ride to view Nevers from above, taking in its mountains and harbours while the wind danced crazily through their hair.

Then came a day when the minivan accidentally drove onto a street full of people. Everything became strangely dark, as though someone had turned a dimmer switch on the city. It gradually occurred to the professor that the darkness was because everyone on the street was dressed entirely in black; even their faces were covered, as though in mourning. There were no other vehicles in sight and the crowd filled both traffic lanes, surging around the van, everyone proceeding slowly in the same direction. Professor Q watched in horror through the van window, noting that some people had gleaming knives stuck in their heads, while others had bandaged eyes, or crudely sewn-up mouths.

Aliss had never seen so many human beings in one place before.

They looked like black water droplets, converging to form a never-ending river. Some of them turned to look at the van; they couldn't see Aliss but Aliss could see them, and to her their eyes were dark vortexes, each vortex a tunnel leading to another secret, expectant city, waiting to bloom wide open like a flower. She reached for them but her hand bumped against the glass. The window was securely locked. Professor Q was scowling and rapping insistently on the partition behind the driver, saying, 'Hurry! Let's go! Let's go!'

The van backed up and turned down a side alley. The crowd vanished behind an enormous tower block. Aliss seemed about to say something, but Professor Q pressed a finger to his lips, instructing her to keep silent. They heard explosions, one then another, and smoke came pouring through the cracks between the buildings. Out of the corner of his eye, Professor Q saw a squadron of green-uniformed military police, and he began to shake uncontrollably.

Professor Q went home early that evening. The flickering television light cast shadows across his face—red, then blue, then all the colours of an exploding firework. The news anchor looked like a porcelain doll, her obliging smile and dulcet tones working wonders on his tormented emotions. In the local news segment, the journalist spent a long time relaying tedious details about a patriotic parade, then finished up with a brief mention of a suicide case that was not being treated as suspicious. No other news was mentioned. The following day, Professor Q went out and bought a local paper, a Valerian-language one that he usually enjoyed, making sure to read every single article. The parade really did seem to be the only significant news. He tossed the paper in the bin as soon as he finished, delighted to think that nothing had actually happened. The only troubling thing was that out on the street he kept seeing grass-green shadows lurking in the periphery of his vision.

To avoid these phantoms, he decided to stop going out. He

closed the church doors and said morosely to Aliss that they had to stay there.

'Come on,' he said. 'Give me a dance.'

At the sight of Aliss dressed up in her swan outfit, his face regained its former liveliness. And the swan was only the beginning: soon it had transformed into a backside as pure as moonlight, and legs that writhed like eels. Cocooned inside his church, the professor forgot all about the dangers of the city. He felt invincible, carefree, and even started to wonder what he was doing keeping such a talented, supremely beautiful goddess of a lover hidden away. Why shouldn't he take her out and show her off?

During those days in the church, Aliss was quiet. She had been designed as a ballerina, yes, but she didn't feel much enthusiasm for dancing. The problem was that once her feet were on stage and the music started up, her body would begin to move automatically, without her volition, and even though she wanted to stop, she couldn't.

As he was leaving the church one evening, Professor Q finally noticed Aliss's dejected expression, but he mistook it for a sign that his ballerina girl felt as heartbroken as he did about their impending separation.

'Oh, Aliss!' he cried. 'My darling girl! I don't want to be apart from you either. Don't worry, soon I'll take you away from here and bring you home with me!'

---- **21** ----

Professor Q could not exactly bring Aliss home with him, but before long the minivan was driving them back into the city, this time to downtown Valeria Island, where it eventually pulled up in front of an old, colonial-style hotel. Professor Q took Aliss's hand in his and together they stepped out of their secret little world.

Aliss had changed into a long, silvery-white dress with a plunging neckline (another gift from Professor Q) and on her feet she wore three-inch heels. Stepping out on a busy Nevers street for the first time, she looked the picture of a blushing bride. People hurried past in all directions. In shop windows, spotlights illuminated glittering wares; Aliss's attention settled briefly on the faceless models in a clothes shop window display, their hands either on their hips or reaching languidly upwards. She turned to look at a glass ball rotating on top of an enormous tower, then at a bejewelled arm reaching down from a billboard towards the street. Sound flooded in from all sides. She would have liked to stay out there for a while longer, taking it all in, but Professor Q hurriedly pulled her into the hotel's entrance.

The revolving glass door swept Aliss into the hotel lobby like a gust of wind. Men in neat suits and ties bowed in greeting. Veins rippled and looped across the shiny lobby floor towards her and, next thing she knew, she and Professor Q were inside a lift that needed a special swipe card to start. She watched as a series of different numbers took turns flashing red.

This romantic escapade had been a long while in the making. Professor Q had been biding his time, waiting for Maria to go out of town on one of her business trips. As soon as she announced an upcoming couple of days away, he had made a reservation at a five-star hotel, choosing the sumptuous honeymoon suite with its panoramic view of Valeria Harbour. Finally, a whole night alone with Aliss!

But there was an important detail to take care of first. Some weeks in advance of the date, Professor Q paid a visit to David's clinic, where one of the flutter-eyed nurses ushered him into a consulting room. Inside, following their usual routine, David selected a popsicle stick and told him to open wide. But Professor Q shook his head, mumbling that today the issue was 'somewhere else'. He made a thumbs-down gesture in the direction of his lower body, his face burning with embarrassment. Unfortunately, David failed to pick up on the cue and simply stared in confusion, obliging Professor Q to lean across the desk between them and whisper in his ear—at which point David had burst out laughing.

The honeymoon suite was at the end of a long corridor. Professor Q opened the door in a state of high excitement, only to find a member of the hotel staff inside, facing away, doing something he could not quite make out. He frowned. The employee seemed startled at the disruption and offered a flustered apology before dashing out of the room. Aliss barely noticed; she was too busy looking around her, thinking how much the room resembled the church. Here, too, an enormous bed occupied the centre of the space, although there was no Jesus nailed to a cross hanging on the wall behind it. Gauzy muslin curtains hung on either side of a pristine window, through which she could see glittering lights. Were those—could those really be—the lights of God?

She walked towards them. The window was actually a door, and this door could be pushed open, leading on to a balcony.

From the balcony, she saw millions of pinpricks of light clustered on either side of the harbour. All the buildings had vanished, transformed into crystal statuettes. She thought of the crowds of human beings on the street outside the minivan the other day. How disappointing not to see them from this height.

Professor Q followed her out, but rather than joining her in admiring the gaudiness of the view, he slipped a hand into his pocket and rooted around, making sure the little blue pill from David was still there. Him and Aliss! The whole night stretched ahead of them, and Professor Q did not intend to let anything stand in the way of making his dreams—at very long last—come true.

Before his thoughts could progress any further, he was surprised by a man with a violin, who suddenly materialized from behind the curtains.

'Congratulations!' said the violinist, leaning into an exaggerated bow. 'As a complimentary service of the honeymoon suite, I am pleased to offer you three songs of your choosing. You may pick whatever you like from this list!'

He whipped out an electronic screen, on which a menu flashed up.

'Oh, we don't need—' began Professor Q, trailing off when he noticed Aliss already engrossed, scrolling delightedly up and down the screen with her fingers.

'If the lady feels so inclined, she could choose a dance tune, and you could dance to the music.'

Professor Q felt uneasy: why had the violinist said 'you' and not 'the two of you'? Could he tell that Aliss was actually a ballerina doll? Something about the man's appearance was familiar, but the professor struggled to remember where he might have seen him before.

As though sensing Professor Q's scrutiny, the violinist smiled in what seemed intended to be a meaningful way. Professor Q felt light-headed; all he wanted to do was lie down on the bed and relax. He retreated inside the room, to the other side of the glass, where he watched silently as the violinist performed for Aliss, who every so often would clap or drum her fingers against the balcony railings.

He had no idea which songs Aliss had asked for. All he could hear from inside the room was the faint squeaking and scraping of the violin, which gave him no clues at all. Feeling bored, he wandered into the bathroom, where he discovered an enormous jacuzzi tub brimming with water and sprinkled with rose petals. A nice hot bath was just what he needed! Without waiting for Aliss, he climbed in, finally beginning to unwind. When the violin noise seemed to have stopped, he called out for Aliss to come in and join him. A head popped around the bathroom door.

'My apologies, Professor,' said the musician. 'I hate to disturb your bath-time tranquillity, but the service is now over and I must take my leave. Before I go, I wonder if I could ask whether you were satisfied with the service? Any comments or suggestions would be gratefully received.'

Understanding the implication, Professor Q waved for the violinist to wait outside the bathroom, then hastily put on a bathrobe and went out to pay a tip. He even felt relatively happy about it because it meant the violinist was finally leaving. Now, surely, he and Aliss would be left alone?

He dimmed the room lighting and placed the blue pill on his tongue, feeling hopeful but also extraordinarily tired.

'Aliss!' he called again.

She was still standing on the balcony, entranced by the ferries making slow trails across Valeria Harbour, and their reflections in the water, and the shimmering multicoloured lights. At the sound of her name, she turned to see Professor Q in his bathrobe, sitting on one side of the bed, leaning back against the headboard. The small reading lamp above him cast a sharp shadow across his face.

She had never noticed before how much he resembled a worn-out mannequin. His face was covered in scratches, both deep and superficial, and his eyes were sunken and dull. His body was limp, as if the springs had come loose. He looked like a discarded toy. She walked over and reached for him, intending to stroke his poor, damaged forehead. But Professor Q grabbed her, pulling her down with a force nothing like that of a broken toy.

He opened his bathrobe as though flinging open a majestic cape. The robe became infinite, stretching over Aliss like a sky. She had crossed into another world, into the small, private world of Professor Q. He had opened the door for her, but behind that door was another door. He opened his mouth, revealing his tongue and all his teeth; he threw off his skin, exposing his bones.

'Come on in, Aliss! No one has ever been so close to me before.'

Aliss walked in, entering a place where things floated and drifted like planets in outer space.

He said, 'That's my heart, that's my liver.'

He took her hand and guided it in a strange new rhythm. He was trying his hardest to show her all his damaged parts. He wanted her to see his rusted gears, his blocked-up pipes.

'Aliss, use your hand! Get all this going again! Or maybe use your long, fleshy legs, yes, that's better. Now use your clever little toes, your ballerina toes! You see? Aliss, oh, Aliss, please, get me going again!'

Some life forms belong to the night. Owls, bats, dreams. By night they soar and by day they retreat into the shadows where no one can see them.

Aliss couldn't be sure whether Owlish was dreaming, but he didn't stir when she crawled out from under the covers beside him. His mouth was closed again, his body locked back up. On her way to the balcony she passed by the dressing table mirror without stopping to look at her reflection. She seemed to have realized her body contained secrets no mirror would ever be able to show her. Outside, the night-time splendour had retreated and the city was now enveloped in fog.

She closed her eyes, enjoying the sensation of the feeble sunlight against her eyelids. It was warm. Could this warmth travel through her eyes to her inner world? Human eyes were such dark vortexes. Was there also an expectant city inside of her, waiting to bloom?

Professor Q had finally opened his eyes, but not yet moved his body or called for Aliss. He watched her naked form from behind, trying to stay inside his dream as long as possible. He felt revitalized, bursting with life, but when he thought of all the things he had been missing out on until this moment, he was flooded with resentment. He didn't want to bring Aliss back to the church. Why should he? Why did they have to keep riding the same mute wooden horse to nowhere, in front of the same damn oil paintings? Why did their pleasure have to be clandestine, sought only at the feet of the merciful Jesus?

He thought of the green-eyed magician. Why couldn't he become a magician and lead around a wandering circus of dolls and toys? On stage, no one would be able to see his face, all they would see were his hands and their magic tricks. He wouldn't belong to any country, or any city, but would instead be in possession of any place his feet carried him to. When Maria came back from her business trip, he would tell her. He would say, 'I've found a new kind of freedom. I've been born again! I want to live a new life!'

In the soft morning light, Aliss's skin shimmered like an aquatic creature. She looked nothing like a doll. She was a newborn human. She was him. Inside, he was eloquent—powerfully, boundlessly eloquent—but as soon as his words reached his lips they transformed into something else. Especially in front of Maria, around whom all his most firmly held convictions were instantly as fragile as soap bubbles. He had drafted so many letters to her, trying to explain the love between him and Aliss. Trying to explain that, no, it wasn't a betrayal, because his pursuing Aliss really amounted to him pursuing himself. Him falling in love with Aliss had nothing to do with his wife; there was absolutely no conflict between the two. He had written these kinds of explanations over and over, the weight of the words seemingly too much for the flimsy sheets of paper to bear. Sometimes he screwed these letters into balls, other times he simply threw them away. Most often he stuffed them into his desk drawer, muttering under his breath, knowing full well that if the drawer were ever opened all the way it would spew the letters back out like an uncontrollable stream of vomit.

22

Maria sat on some stone steps by a pier, looking at boats anchored in the bay. The sea kept throwing up swathes of sickly foam; every so often, a ferry horn let loose a long wail. The sky was overcast. Beyond the scene immediately in front of her, the city was completely obscured by fog.

She had travelled by bus to the Outlying Destination Ferry Pier. Once there, however, she had not proceeded to the departure hall. Instead, she had tried to reach Professor Q by phone, to tell him that all ferries to City H had been cancelled on account of the fog. As she had expected, the call did not go through.

It was too late in the day to return to the office, but she decided not to head straight home. The ferry cancellation hadn't come as much of a surprise. As she sat there on the steps, all she could think about was the night before. She had struggled to fall asleep and, at a certain point, she realized that her husband had crept into the bedroom without turning on the light, and that he was groping around in the darkness like a ghost, kicking and banging into things in his search for the bed.

When he eventually made it, she felt as though she could see his body lying motionless beside her. But the room was pitch-dark and she had her back to him; what she was seeing was the moon, gnawed down to a cryptic smirk. She thought about saying something, but silence hung between them like a protective film and she couldn't bring herself to pierce it.

The stench from the sea felt suddenly overwhelming, although no one else seemed to mind. People were strolling along the promenade with their dogs, beaming with happiness. What was she waiting around for? The same scene kept repeating itself over and over; time did not seem to be moving in a linear direction. Eventually another ferry horn sounded and she got up, gathered her luggage, and caught another bus.

As the bus entered her neighbourhood, she started to feel less anxious. Railings extended seamlessly along the length of the pavements. Green men lit up at pedestrian crossings and cars stopped obediently behind the painted lines. Perfectly spherical bushes offset perfectly trapezoidal flowerbeds. Even the ubiquitous security guards, in their sky-blue uniforms, had a soothing effect.

It was a self-contained, self-satisfied little world. Anything irregular was forced outside its borders: the rock musicians and rusting drains in far-off abandoned warehouses, the mumbling vagrants clattering through tunnels trailing strings of empty drink cans, the blue-skinned foreigners holding up convenience stores at knifepoint, the Ksanese tourists picking fights with locals. As a well-educated resident of the neighbourhood, Maria of course paid attention to what was happening in the world outside of it—from time to time those people and their goings-on would unexpectedly find their way into the newspapers, reported on in that abnormal, flattened language that only exists in written form.

More often, however, Maria simply had no way of knowing about such trifling matters, no way of realizing those people even existed, because the articles were usually printed in Southern-language newspapers and she liked to read her news in Valerian. The Valerian papers concerned themselves with international news, with the much more serious stories of major world events. Southern was a fickle, elusive language, full of emotion, and Maria much pre-ferred Valerian's fixed noun cases and verb conjugations, and the clear boundaries between its nouns and adjectives. When the world was arranged according to this linguistic structure, everything be-came clearer: time, place, cause and effect, gender. It made the world neat and tidy, a place with a clearly defined inside and outside, read-ily comprehensible.

She thought of a blue student handbook from her primary school days, which she used to hold reverently with both hands, reading meticulously from left to right, delighting in the numbered rules and quantifiable objectives. She liked to work through the book with a tiny pencil, wielding it like a needle, carefully sewing together all the tiny loopholes, making sure the language was per-fectly airtight. Now, on the bus back from the ferry terminal, she noticed another hole. In her fiercely controlled surroundings, some-thing had been damaged: there was a hissing noise, as though air was rapidly escaping.

Her key turned crisply in the front door, as it always did. It was noon, but the lack of sun made everything inside the apartment look undefined. Shadows cast by the furniture flickered weakly across the floor; for a brief moment Maria wondered if they were trying to talk to her, but she couldn't hear anything. She set down her suit-case and walked through the living room to the balcony, intending to bring in Professor Q's coat, which had been out there drying for the past two days. When she touched the fabric, it was still soak-ing wet. It was no wonder: for aesthetic reasons, the building man-agement did not allow laundry to be hung on the sunny side of the block. Not that anywhere in the city had seen much of the sun re-cently anyway.

She sat down on the sofa. From that position, she had a clear view of the closed bathroom door. She pictured Professor Q walking out from behind it: in recent months, he always left the bathroom with his hair slicked back, his body doused in cologne, his mouth minty fresh. He shaved his face smooth each morning and had abandoned his shapeless, sludge-toned sweaters in favour of pink shirts with flamboyantly embroidered cuffs. As she imagined him sauntering past, she noticed how snugly his trendy new jeans fitted against his sagging behind.

She scowled. The outfit was ridiculous. He looked nothing like a respectable university professor! He looked like an out-of-touch old creep heading off to chase his next big thrill. But he didn't look unfamiliar, exactly. She was thinking of a particular day—what was it that had happened? It was years ago, and they had been discussing something or, at least, she had been explaining an opinion she had about something, and Q had suddenly shaken his head and, without saying a word, lain down on some train tracks. She had screamed, but her scream had been instantly drowned out by the horn of the approaching train. That was the image of Q she had seared into her memory: him lying there, accompanied by the ear-piercing shriek of train wheels grating against their tracks. It was a stubborn, forceful noise, which blocked out all other sound, as though they had reached the absolute limit of incomprehension.

She had assumed Q's crazy streak was tamed long ago, but now it was occurring to her that the Q who had lain down on the train tracks had not, in fact, disappeared; he had just been gradually obscured by layer upon layer of accumulated fat, until he was completely trapped inside a sagging, human-shaped flesh suit. Professor Q spent all day reading, seemingly nourished by nightmarishly abstruse theses and the kind of hallucinatory fiction it gave Maria headaches just to think about. If she pressed an ear to that everexpanding belly of his, perhaps she would still be able to hear the shrieking of the train wheels, buried so deep now that the sound would struggle to filter through. For as long as she could remember,

she had yearned for an old age that resembled the thin end of a fun-
nel: the possibility of anything unexpected happening would shrink
to almost zero and memories would drip out reassuringly, one at a
time, into glass bottles, which could then be neatly sealed up and put
away on shelves where the contents could no longer harm anyone.

Beside the three-seater sofa on which Maria sat was the armchair where Professor Q usually liked to read. Even when he was
not physically there, Maria still had the feeling the chair belonged
exclusively to him. While he was sitting in the chair, he would
sometimes put down his book and stare off through the small, sea-
facing window. In these moments, despite the two of them being
only inches apart, Maria always felt that he had gone somewhere
very far away. It was as if his immobile form had undergone some
kind of vaporization process, allowing the real him to transcend his
stiff human shell and walk outside onto the street, passing silently
along the neighbourhood's neat, straight roads and their carefully
erected pedestrian railings, continuing until he burst through to a
forbidden realm—and no matter how loudly she shouted, she was
powerless to stop him.

In truth, she rarely tried. Seeing him there, sunken into another
world, she felt compelled to hold her breath and tiptoe gingerly
around him. Something leaden seemed to be growing even heavier,
and the lightest of touches risked turning it into a monster; one misstep and their home, along with the calm, steady lives they lived inside it, would end up warped, like metal boxes left in the sun too
long, junk just like all the other junk the city was overflowing with.
There was no space left to throw anything away.

Maria noticed the door to Professor Q's study was cracked open,
and a line of light crept out from behind it, extending across the
floor to her toes. She took it as a silent invitation: rousing herself,
she went to her store cupboard to fetch a cloth and some cleaning
products.

The room was bright and airy, just as she had always longed for it to be, cleared of her husband's books and clutter. One slim book remained on his desk. A book that, as she drew closer, turned out not to be a book at all, but a women's fashion magazine. The cover showed a young woman in profile with flowers piled on top of her head, the effect being a kind of orb of blossoms. Her long, white neck looked like the neck of a bottle. One of those vacuous fashion girls? No, her features were too arresting and her gaze too sharp; there was definitely something sentient there.

Maria never bought fashion magazines. Out of curiosity, she started to leaf through, discovering full-colour pages of models in strange outfits, arranged in positions that struck her as absolutely shameless. But before she could dwell too long on these obscenities, she came across something inserted between the pages. It was a stack of receipts and itemized credit card bills, detailing expenses for clothes, underwear, and a hotel room—a honeymoon suite, no less, and on dates that just so happened to coincide with her intended work trip to City H. The paper trembled a little in her hands. She kept turning pages until she arrived at another insertion, this time a folded-over letter that, once opened, turned out to be addressed to her. She read through, scrutinizing every word. It was unfinished and the language was terrible, babbling nonsense, but the message was clear and sharp as a knife.

Her head pounded with fury, while her arms and legs went limp. She returned to the living room and collapsed on the sofa. The oblivious phantasm of Professor Q was still sitting in the armchair opposite. With great effort, Maria managed to make her arm throw the cleaning rag at him, and it was then she heard the hissing again. It sounded both close by and very far away, coming from somewhere inside her body that she had no ability to access. She compressed herself, hugging her knees tightly to her chest, trying to stop the air from leaking out. Her whole body was shaking. Shaking and, no, that wasn't air leaking out, it was tears, trickling from her eyes. Maybe she should have done something to stop them, to get things under control, but she didn't. She let herself sit there, feeling all that was round and plump and perfect inside her body gradually shrivel up.

23

Love heightened Professor Q's powers of imagination. It emboldened him. When he took Aliss's hand and led her out of their hotel room in the morning, the hallway seemed different from before. How to put it? The room numbers and carpet were now bathed in a celestial light, and he had the distinct feeling of walking along a church aisle, with pews on either side and a priest at the far end standing in front of an altar. He imagined that the violinist from the previous night had reappeared to play the wedding march; perhaps not the best of musicians, but he would do. Of course, this was not a real marriage ceremony. It couldn't be, because that would have made Professor Q a bigamist. But Professor Q had clean forgotten he was already a married man. The idea of a religious ceremony may have seemed a little absurd, but every now and then even absurdities have their logic, and that morning he had woken up filled with religious fervour. If anything in the world was sacred, it was surely this: a love that transcended age, transcended background, even transcended species.

Whose voice was it that now rang in his ears? Owlish? The magician from the auction?

And now, with the Lord God as our witness, do . . . you . . . accept Aliss into your home? In this world of humans, do you take her, a being of another species entirely, for richer or for poorer, for better or for worse, in sickness and in health?

'Yes! I do! I do!'

If any man be in love, he is a new creature: old things are passed away; behold, all things are become new.

Numbers throbbed on a small screen as the lift ascended from the mortal world to the heavens, flinging its doors wide to admit Professor Q and his companion. He was delighted to see no one else inside it, just a luxurious shagpile carpet and a glimmering mirrored ceiling in which he saw a world turned upside down.

Sadly, the rest of the hotel was of the earthly plane, and before long the lift had stopped at another floor where a couple entered. The man was taller than the professor, and wearing a better-quality suit. He glanced briefly at Aliss but refused to meet Professor Q's eye. The jewel-encrusted woman with him, however, stared unapologetically at both Aliss and the professor, clearly taking note of every detail. Professor Q tried to retaliate, intending to frighten her off with a scowl, but his face refused to cooperate; it remained stiff and impassive, and he found himself shrinking into a corner. He tried in vain to give Aliss a reassuring smile.

From then on, the lift seemed to stop at every floor, the number of people inside it steadily increasing. Professor Q and Aliss ended up pushed to the back, but the eyes of these newcomers always found them. Professor Q felt his throat tighten and sweat trickle down his back. The fingers of the hand with which he gripped Aliss began to quiver.

When the lift finally reached the ground floor, Professor Q was impatient to remove himself and Aliss from that anxiety-inducing little box. But as the lift-riders ahead of him started to thin, he spotted someone he recognized outside in the lobby. The person was sitting in the hotel coffee lounge with his back to the lift doors, chatting to a grey-haired man who gave the impression of being very important; every wrinkle on his face seemed to gleam with authority. It was Professor W's back, there was no doubt about it. The other man looked vaguely familiar too—was perhaps some high-level university official, or else a politician.

The crowd from the lift dispersed, leaving Professor Q and Aliss exposed, at risk of being seen by anyone who cared to look. He glanced at her, his expression tender, but a moment later he had shaken off her hand and marched into the lobby alone. Keeping his head down, he strode quickly in the direction of the reception desk, stopping when he reached a marble pillar large enough to hide behind.

From behind the pillar, he had a clear view of the coffee lounge. W and his VIP seemed to be getting on like a house on fire. Who was that man? And how had W come to know him, let alone on such cosy terms? Clearly, Professor Q had underestimated the faculty's latest, most junior hire, and all that earnest, may-I-ask-your-advice stuff had been nothing but show. Was there any chance W had seen him with Aliss? Who knew what rumours might fly in the university if he was seen sneaking around a hotel with a pretty young girl (or, indeed, a pretty young foreigner doll).

His legs were shaking, not with fear—or so he told himself—so much as with the sheer force of emotions coursing through his body. The longer he observed the two men, the more convinced he became that they had not noticed him, and he began to calm down. But then another thought struck him: where had Aliss got to? He looked around, pleased to see that she had not tried to chase after him or yell his name in the middle of the lobby, which would only have attracted attention. However, there was no sign of her at all. Where could she have gone?

Fortunately, Professor W and his companion were at that moment signalling for their coffee bill. Professor Q sidled around his pillar, taking great pains to ensure he remained out of their line of vision as they paid and moved away from the lounge, towards the revolving doors. Once they had left, he stepped out and began straightening his clothes, noticing as he did so that a doorman was eyeing him suspiciously. He made a point of smiling back and walked over to the reception desk, where he loudly announced his room number and desire to check out. When he glanced back to see the doorman's reaction, the doorman had vanished.

The receptionist silently typed in Professor Q's details, then handed him a print-out of his receipt and moved on to the next guest. He already knew how much the room would cost, but it was still a shock to see the numbers in black and white. And, despite the fact he was spending all that money, the hotel staff seemed determined not to take him seriously. He had half a mind to complain about the violinist, but decided against it. Not because he was intimidated, he told himself, but because his priority was finding Aliss.

No one said a word to him as he paced around the lobby. In fact, he had the feeling they were all looking right through him: the guests in the coffee lounge, the guests on the sofas by the main entrance, the doormen, the reception staff. Their faces were like sheets of steel, reflecting back on one another, all of them apparently in agreement that Professor Q was surplus to the city's requirements, a nobody they could crush with one finger.

Cutting through Professor Q's indignation was a mounting sense of panic about having lost Aliss. He returned to the lift and saw from the light-up display that it had stopped on the top floor. This gave him a flicker of hope—perhaps Aliss had gone back to the room? He frantically pressed the call button. When the lift finally arrived, discharging another crowd of guests, he forced his way inside and found Aliss still there, standing in the corner where he had left her. She had a smile on her face and one of her arms was outstretched, its palm curled as though beckoning him over. He went to take her hand in his, overcome with joy. But when he tried to lead her out, she wouldn't come. That's right: Aliss had frozen. Professor Q looked again at her face. How had he failed to notice that, although the corners of her mouth were upturned, as if smiling, the rest of her face was rigid? Her outstretched arm would not fold back. Her whole body was rigid.

Our poor professor! Now not only did he have to pick up Aliss, who was no insignificant weight, he also had to endure the stares as he performed the incredible spectacle of carrying a—what was it? a woman? a woman-sized doll?—through the hotel lobby to the entrance. Luckily for him, the minivan was waiting outside. He asked the driver to help lift Aliss in, then climbed in himself and closed the doors, his heart rate finally starting to slow.

He hugged Aliss to him, looking intently at her face. Her eyes were closed, as if asleep. Perhaps inspired by how these scenes usually go in fairy tales, he leaned down and started kissing her, his aged skin chafing against her cheeks. Rather than bringing Aliss back to life, the kisses sent chills through his body.

He laid Aliss on the sofa and retreated to a corner. Aliss, oh Aliss, he thought, was it all just one big illusion? He was an old man, already fifty. Owlish had said, *This could be your last chance for adventure.* Was this it? Had he let his last chance slip away?

Surely not. What Aliss needed was a good night's sleep, then she would be herself again. She had never talked or walked as much as she had in the last couple of days, and she had probably just overexerted herself. When she woke up, he would explain his plan, explain to her that he was going to tell Maria everything.

All the way back to the church, while his thoughts raced, Professor Q kept one hand on the doll on the sofa, holding her firm against bumps in the road. To keep her warm, he covered her with one of the suit jackets he had bought her, and her outstretched arm stuck out from underneath the fabric as though attempting to pluck something from the air. At the sight of it, he couldn't resist gripping her open palm and whispering in her ear: 'Aliss! Aliss!'

But although Aliss's ears were open and her mouth was smiling, not a word escaped her lips.

24

On Sunday morning, beams of sunlight climbed the soles of Maria's feet, entering their every pore, making them glow like consecrated objects. Maria looked down at her toes. They were silent, their outlines sharp, with nice clear spaces in between each one. What had she done all day yesterday? Nothing much, aside from opening up the contacts list on her phone and making a few calls.

She sat up on the sofa and stared through the window at the street outside. The sunshine was genuine, she concluded. The clouds had really parted, and now sunlight was flooding through.

Her gaze drifted towards the door of Professor Q's study and she wondered if his coat had dried. Then she stopped herself: what did she care about his coat? There were more important things to be getting on with. She went into the study and hunted through the paperwork inside the fashion magazine, looking for the name of the hotel.

For the rest of the morning, she hovered around the hotel entrance. At first she loitered in a shadowy corner of the car park, then she went to hide behind a lamp post. Any time she noticed someone looking at her, she changed position, trying to keep out of sight. She felt ashamed, convinced that everyone else knew more about what her husband was up to than she did, yet somehow it was she who was the object of their hostility.

Finally, she saw him. He came through the hotel doors with a glossy-haired foreign woman in his arms—no, not a foreign woman. Maria could not believe her eyes. The body he was carrying had both feet off the ground and one arm sticking out to the side, palm flat, as though ready to shake hands with passers-by. And it was not a woman's body, it was a doll's. A toy! The doll's chin rested on his shoulder. It was facing Maria, eyes wide and guileless, mouth angled into a smile—a genuine smile, seemingly without a trace of malice. Maria watched as a man stepped out of the driver's seat of a minivan and helped her husband lift the doll on board.

She leapt into a taxi, instructing the driver to follow the van. The two vehicles drove out beyond the city limits, leaving behind the districts Maria knew and turning onto increasingly narrow, unpaved roads, skidding across gravel, splattering their paintwork with mud. At one point, the taxi wheels became stuck in a patch of mud, and she worried they would have to give up. After several angry revs of the engine, the car shot free, but it was the final straw for the driver, who started cursing about being tricked into driving out to such a godforsaken place, with no idea how to get back home.

Maria tried to pacify him, promising to double his rate, while also struggling to keep her own anxiety in check. The battle continued until Professor Q's minivan drew up to a small pier. Beyond the pier, water extended as far as the eye could see, undisturbed aside from a few scattered fishing boats. Professor Q carried his doll out of the van, boarded a waiting boat, and within seconds had set sail for the horizon. Without pausing to think, Maria found a fisherman and pointed wordlessly after them. The fisherman picked up his oars.

With a salty wind blowing in her face, Maria clung tightly to the side of the boat. Once her breathing had calmed, she peered over and noted the phenomenal clarity of the water, in which she could see flurries of shadowy little fish. The departed smog had left the sky a surreal blue, the line of the distant horizon broken only by a single, emerald-green island. On a different day, in a different mood, Maria would have loved it. She thought of all the books she had read about Nevers geography and ecology, and felt profoundly ashamed that she had no idea where she was.

Then her mind turned to the strange map that had appeared in her email inbox. What if this was the area it had slated for redevelopment? She turned to look behind her, towards the shore, where a wispy cloud lingered over a far-off mountain, only adding to her sense that it was all a mirage.

Professor Q's boat docked at the emerald-green island, and Maria watched as he disembarked and began to carry his doll up a flight of stone steps. She hurried off her own boat to follow him, realizing partway up the steps that, astonishingly, they led to a pristine, dove-white church.

When she reached the church entrance, the doors were locked. She circled the building. The windows were blacked out, but at the bottom of the back wall there was a small opening, about as wide as a wrist, presumably once an outlet for some kind of pipe. A long way past caring about appearances, Maria crouched down and pressed an eye to the hole, through which she had a clear view of the church interior.

An elaborate rocking horse, a double-seater leopard-print desk chair, an enormous four-poster bed with curtains draped around it . . . every item inside the church came as a shock. And there among them was her husband, the life-sized human doll still in his arms, heading in the direction of her spyhole.

He laid the doll on the altar and started to take off its clothes. Maria covered her mouth with her hands. She did not have a clear view of the doll, but she could see perfectly her husband and the look of crazed determination on his face. Once the doll was naked, he leaned over it with a minuscule pair of pointed forceps—and at this point Maria squeezed her eyes shut, unable to look. When she opened them again, he seemed to be acting more tenderly, carefully inspecting each of the doll's limbs. Then he propped it up and began to move the body parts around, looking every inch like a little boy playing house with his toys.

After a while, he seemed to give up. He dressed the doll in a lacy white tutu and then carried it over to a dressing table where he combed its tangled hair into a smooth topknot and adorned it with a glittering swan headpiece. Maria watched for so long that her legs went numb from holding the same position, but she still couldn't fathom what perverted idea her husband had in mind. For a long time, he just stood there. Eventually he moved the doll to the desk chair and produced a large book of glossy colour photos, using one hand to hold up the doll and the other to turn the pages. His mouth was pressed against the doll's ear, murmuring something unintelligible, the effect that of a doting father explaining a story to his beloved daughter. Maria felt all her anger and sadness vanish, replaced instead with shock and bewilderment. These feelings only deepened when, a few minutes later, she watched her husband close the book, bury his face in the doll's shoulder, and burst into tears.

25

When had the summer charged in? It suddenly felt poisonously hot, the sunlight sharpened to a fine blade, the cut-throat, silvery shrieks of cicadas attacking from all sides. Professor Q's nerves were painfully taut. His lover, once so sweet and tender, was now back inside her music box, a cold, stiff, wordless toy.

He went to sit on the two-seater chair at the desk, hoping to regain his concentration. Unfortunately for him, the first thing he laid hands on was a notebook containing an essay he had drafted a few days before, refuting the ideas of Immanuel Kant. From the opening lines, it was clearly bullshit. Utter bullshit! He read through the notebook, skimming things he had written in previous months, and the further back he went the greater his conviction that it was all nonsense, embarrassing, the ramblings of a madman. He couldn't believe he had written any of it, let alone fantasized about publishing it one day. His sadness faded, replaced by disgust—although whether it was disgust at his whereabouts or at himself, he couldn't say.

He stormed out of the church. The wretched hilltop was drenched in sunlight, but the trees cast ink-black shadows and the air was full of mysterious insect cries. The effect was inebriating; nothing was quite as it seemed. He set off down a path without any idea where he was going, soon finding himself back on the ridge that looked out towards the big grey office block where he worked. The building itself was as ugly as ever but the sunlight was making it sparkle, almost as if its hideousness made it more worthy of the attention. Something odd was happening—the building was drab yet sparkling, and it was planted solidly into the ground yet seemed, somehow, to be readying for a fight. The summer holidays had started, who would even be in the office now? Professor W's face flashed to mind. Professor Q pressed a hand to his eyes. After all those weeks of smog, sun now burned across the city like wildfire. It was scorching! Was it some kind of warning? Terror spread through the professor like a flame eating the fuse on a powder keg, until it consumed him completely.

Next thing he knew, Professor Q was back on the Lone Boat campus. Truth be told, he was not at all clear on why he had decided to come. It was a long time since his last visit, and he had assumed the summer holidays would mean the campus was empty, but when his taxi pulled through the main gates he saw the place was crawling with uniformed security personnel, and he noticed big, meaty men in jeans and t-shirts lurking in corners, law enforcement writ large across their faces. As he peered at them through the taxi window, his body began to tremble.

The taxi dropped him in front of his office block, where he could feel eyes boring into his back. He kept his head down and fumbled to input his security code, throwing himself through the doors as soon as his entry was approved. Once inside, he could catch his breath a little. He retreated to a part of the lobby out of the sun's reach, and from there he tried to see through the glass entrance doors to the person spying on him, but all he saw was a nearby azalea bush quivering in the breeze.

When he reached his floor, he was almost surprised to find everything as he had left it. Gold-embossed name plaques still hung on each professor's office door; the same stale odour lingered in the corridor; the lines of transparent staff mailboxes remained stubbornly in place. The only difference was a letter lying in his own mailbox, a red 'CONFIDENTIAL' stamped on its envelope. The letter had been issued by the university's Special Task Committee (a committee he had not even known existed) and, without giving any further details, it requested his presence at 3:30 p.m. that afternoon in the central administration building, for a special interview.

He wondered what would have happened if he hadn't come on campus that day. Would he have simply missed the appointment?

The letter did not say who was requesting his presence, nor what they wanted to talk about, but an interview in the central administration building could only be about something important. Perhaps the student strike? But why were they calling it an 'interview' rather than a meeting? Didn't an interview somehow imply that he would be the target of the discussion rather than a participant? Had he inadvertently done something wrong? Of course, there could be a more cheerful explanation. And at least he had picked up the letter in time not to miss this so-called interview. Perhaps it was an interview to praise his performance, not to reprimand him—that happened sometimes, didn't it? He had been at the university for over a decade, after all. The department head could have put in a good word for him with the higher-ups, drawing their attention to his valuable contributions to the university, and now perhaps they had decided not to make him go through the formal evaluation process all over again, and instead were going to bring forward his promotion to associate professor and offer him tenure. But if this was so, why hadn't the department head given him some kind of hint, allowing him to go in prepared?

He went into his office and sat down in his ergonomic chair, sinking back, trying to relax, but almost immediately he sensed that something about the room was different. What was it? The blinds were down, so nobody could have been watching him through the window. Was it the lack of music? Maybe a bit of music would calm him down? No, it wasn't about music—it was the wall in front of him. It was too white. Something used to hang there and now it was gone, leaving behind only a nail and the fine cracks that radiated from the nail into the wall around it. Who had taken the painting? Surely a thief wouldn't care about such a worthless piece of art?

Professor Q stared at the nail, attempting to recall what the painting had looked like. He had a vague recollection of its colours, but aside from that his memory was blank. The nail looked brand new. Could it be that he had put in the nail and forgotten to hang the painting? But then where was the painting he had been intending to hang? He checked his phone. It was barely noon. What was he going to do with the next three hours? He contemplated his hands, turning them over to see the palms, suddenly feeling that the lines there were imbued with deep significance. Each palm seemed to conceal a map, not of a specific place but rather a disguised version of the world's essence. The webs created by those criss-crossing lines seemed complex, but in reality they all arrived at the same destination, demonstrating the inevitability of fate. If he could gather enough samples, perhaps a study of human palm lines would lead him to a groundbreaking truth undiscovered by any previous scholar?

Professor Q would not have been able to explain how he whiled away the next couple of hours, but he was pleased with his decision to finally leave his office, even if there was still some time to go before his appointment. Outside, there was nobody around and the sun was beating ferociously against the concrete. Professor Q followed the winding path uphill. He had heard about the central administrative building but never known exactly where it was. According to the signs, he needed to go all the way to the top of the Lone Boat hill, a part of campus he had never been to before.

He passed the bronze statue of the Confucian scholar, noting that the metal barriers around it had been removed. The Confucian looked the same as ever. It was all right for him! He was already departed, there was nothing left for him to fear. That face, that smirk—they would never change. The Confucian was with the spirits now, what did he care about the living? How could he possibly understand what it was like for poor, luckless Professor Q? The Confucian had founded the university but it was clear from his expression that he despised it, along with everyone in it. Professor Q felt resentful, although of whom exactly he did not know. His legs were tired. He took a deep breath and continued on.

To his surprise, the grandly named central administrative building turned out be a squat, single-storey construction even less assuming than his own drab office block. As he drew nearer, he noticed that the entrance, in particular, was nowhere near as stately as he had imagined. The low-ceilinged, windowless lobby resembled a run-down subway station, with the same inadequate lighting and even a security gate barring his access. Squinting through the gloom, he saw a security guard napping in one corner. He called out politely, then waved, but when the guard failed to react he gave in and shouted, leaping up and down as he did so until his shouts became more like roars. Reluctantly, the guard stood up and shuffled over.

'I'm . . .'

'ID?'

Professor Q had been hoping one mention of the Special Task Committee would be enough, but the guard was unimpressed. He refused even to meet the professor's eyes, and instead stared listlessly into the distance, idly scratching his neck. There was nothing for it: the professor had to bring out his letter, despite its large, red CONFIDENTIAL stamp.

The guard opened the letter, raising and lowering his eyebrows as he read. It was unlikely he could read Valerian, thought Professor Q; the whole thing was probably an elaborate pretence. Regardless, he obeyed the guard's instructions to enter a lift. Once inside, he noticed that all the floor numbers were negative. So that was it! The building had been constructed on a slope, and the floor he had entered on was actually the top level. Now, he would descend to the underworld.

When the lift doors parted, a woman Professor Q recognized as the faculty dean's secretary was waiting outside. He was about to greet her but she refused to meet his eyes, instead leading him directly into a large conference room taken up by an enormous oval table, at the far end of which were three men in suits. Professor Q squinted across the expanse of tabletop, trying to make out who these men were. One was his head of department and, to his horror, the other two looked a lot like the faculty dean and the university president. Could that possibly be right? The more he squinted, the blurrier the faces became.

'Good afternoon, Professor Q. Please sit down,' said the head of department. He was talking into a microphone, presumably because the room was so big, and even these perfectly ordinary remarks took on the gravitas of a speech.

'Do you know why we have invited you here today?'

Professor Q shook his head and scrambled to take a seat, avoiding the microphone that had been set in front of him.

'You must have heard about the recent theft of the president's portrait?'

The department head's voice seemed excessively loud. Professor Q rubbed his ears. Theft? The tone of the question suggested this incident was common knowledge, but he knew nothing about it. He shook his head again.

The department head turned to confer with the other two men. Professor Q's back was sweating; he screwed up his eyes some more, trying to bring the men into focus, but all he saw were ghostly outlines.

'In that case,' said the department head, after a long interval, 'could we ask whether you have recently entered into a relationship with someone previously unknown to you?'

Professor Q flushed. This time his response was immediate: he shook his head, even more vigorously than before.

'There's no hurry, take your time. Perhaps the name "Aliss" might help jog your memory?'

The shock Professor Q had felt on arrival now extended through his whole body. He began to shake violently. The head of department knew about Aliss? All manner of pornographic scenes flooded his mind. Had someone been following him this entire time? But he was a nobody, a complete unknown, why would the university care what he got up to in his private life? And why would they make such a big deal about it? He could see the secretary out of the corner of his eye, standing to one side of the room, her expression blank—so much so that you could say she had no expression at all. Did she know about Aliss too?

At this point, he noticed a security camera on the ceiling near where he was sitting, its lens trained aggressively on him. Was this how the men seemed to be attuned to his every move, while he couldn't see the first thing about them?

'It seems you might finally have remembered something.'

Professor Q looked up at the camera, then back in the direction of the three men.

'You know, we invited you here for your own good. We want to help you. Perhaps it will aid your recollections if I remind you that, according to our records, you have been at the university for over ten years, during which period you have twice applied for tenure, both times without success. I believe you are intending to make a third application this year.'

'But . . .' Professor Q seemed to lose control of himself a little. 'I don't understand. What does any of that have to do with Aliss?'

'Please use your microphone!'

Professor Q ignored the department head's command, distracted by the hushed conversation taking place between the other two men. Meanwhile, the secretary pulled a photo from a stack of documents and set it on the table in front of him.

'Does this painting look familiar to you?'

He recognized the painting in the photo immediately. Or, at least, he thought he did. Wasn't it the one that had gone missing from his office? No, on second glance, it was very similar to the one from his office (the style was identical) but the two figures seemed to have been reversed. Yes, that was it: the male figure was no longer a silhouette but a fully visible, fleshed-out person, and the ballerina had been reduced to a dark outline. Most unsettling of all, the man looked an awful lot like him.

'Let us be frank with one another, Professor Q. We have reason to believe that the painter of this artwork played a significant role in the disappearance of the president's portrait. We also believe they painted the piece you had hanging in your office. For the time being, we are not accusing you of any involvement, but we do request your cooperation. Tell us who the painter is.'

Professor Q hesitated, then picked up his microphone.

'Listen, whatever you might be thinking, I have no idea what you're talking about. This painting looks familiar to me because I happen to have been sent a very similar one. I would like someone to tell *me* who painted it! Think about it, if I knew the painting could be used as proof of some kind of crime, why would I have hung it up in the first place?'

'Professor Q, I don't know who you are trying to protect. Let me assure you, however, that sooner or later the truth will come to light. Both the police and the university are investigating. We consider you one of us, we're on the same side. We'll give you a few days to think this over. Perhaps if you go away and think about it, you'll come back with something to report.'

Before the professor could respond, the secretary had snatched away his microphone. She was getting her revenge! Nothing made sense; he wanted to ask her for some kind of justification, but she was already gesturing for him to leave.

Bam! He watched the door slam shut, feeling as if his head had suddenly been emptied.

Had any of it really happened? Professor Q smarted at the injustice. He had no idea how he had ended up back at the top of the Lone Boat University hill. With the sunlight receding around him, he chose a secluded spot to sit and reflect on what had just unfolded. Glistening teardrops bobbed across the surface of Cloudy Harbour. How had things reached this point? Why did the university have any idea about the artwork he chose to hang in his office? Once again, Professor W's face came to mind. His appearance in the hotel that morning couldn't have been an accident. Professor Q reached for his phone and opened the department website, scrolling until he landed on W's grinning profile. Then he remembered the violinist who had materialized out of nowhere in the hotel room, and then— then—the clown from the antiques street.

From among these faces, another one took shape, framed by messy hair, with long, slender, birdlike eyes. Owlish! Of course. Who else could help him now? He carefully entered those five digits into his phone, the keypad emitting a beep and a flash of light with each press. This was an SOS, his lifeline, a spell to ward off demons. Except— well, except the line remained silent. Nothing happened. How was it possible? It had connected before, why wasn't it connecting now?

An hour later, he was at the sales desk of a telecommunications shop, repeating the situation to a pitying young retail assistant. The assistant glanced at the number Professor Q had written down and, smiling, with as much patience as he could muster, explained that the situation was only to be expected.

'With all due respect, sir,' he said, 'nowadays Nevers phone numbers are eight digits long.'

The assistant looked barely out of high school. Professor Q did not appreciate his tone. Obviously he knew Nevers phone numbers were eight digits long! Did he look like a fool? The point was that the five-digit number had worked the last time he tried it. The boy's smile looked so fake that the professor felt inclined to reach out and rip it off his face. But wait, that smile was familiar. Where had he seen it before? He snatched his phone from the assistant's hands and ran out of the shop as fast as his legs would carry him.

26

Let us leave our madman Professor Q for a moment and turn instead to his church. To his church, and to Aliss, Aliss-the-toy, curled inside her music box, knees to her chest like an unhatched chick. It was the pose she knew best, the one she seemed to have been doing all her life: making herself as small as possible to endure the darkness. Except this time you could say she had truly become the unhatched chick. The outside of her body was hardening into a shell. It was not that she hadn't heard Professor Q's pleading, it was that this developing shell had rendered her immobile, as though suddenly turned to stone, unable to move so much as a finger.

Her fingers were where it had started. After her hand was so ruthlessly discarded, the petrification had crept from her fingertips into the rest of her body. *You don't yet know the ways of the world. You have no idea of its dangers.* Professor Q's damp voice echoed in her ear. She didn't know what she was made of, but it had to be something lighter than stone—she used to feel almost weightless, as though empty inside. But in the corner of the hotel lift, after everyone else had left and the metallic doors had slotted together like two perfect blades, her legs seemed to turn to marble.

She could not be transforming into a statue, this much she knew for sure. Because although her limbs had gone heavy, a charge had started to radiate from somewhere deep inside her. She wanted to open her mouth and shout, but her pipes were stopped up, trapping her voice inside her body, where it kept on swelling.

In Professor Q's absence, everything in the church, from the furniture to the books, the assorted collected objects, all of their shadows, had reverted to their truest states of being, and a different sound had taken over, a sort of chirping. A chirping of cicadas, birds, frogs, wind, sunlight, dust. Each had their own language, none of which Aliss could yet understand, but she felt as though she did; they seemed to be talking on her behalf. Their voice was her voice, clambering like a vine over the church interior. Her lips parted and her fingers began to tremble. To her surprise, she found that she could lift her arms—only slightly, but enough to crack open the music box lid.

Through the narrow opening, she could see early evening sunlight seeping along the edges of the black window coverings. The light entered not in multicoloured beams but in pale gold threads, giving the effect of barely opened eyes peering into her sealed-off universe. The eyes were directed to the figure in the middle of the church's holiest place, nailed high on his cross, head drooping to one side, face screwed up in anguish. She had never paid him much attention before. Beneath his contorted wooden features, she now saw intersecting streams. They gushed violently across his forehead and down his neck, over his prominent rib cage, his thighs, his calves, all the way to his ankles. His feet were crossed one on top of the other and held in place with an enormous nail, the same kind of nail that was hammered through the palm of each of his wide-open, trembling hands.

Aliss suspected that streams were coursing through her body too. She could feel them roiling inside her, determined to find a way out. *The Love that moves the sun and all the other stars.* She had read that line in a book. Drifting dust motes congregated along the threads of sunlight, forming rivers in mid-air. Was that the Love that moved them? If light could pierce through human skin, and through her skin, what would she see? She remembered Owlish holding her in his arms, and how his whole body had quivered. Inside of him, there must also have been a stream determined to find a way out.

Where was the line between a human being and a doll that could move? Back in the magician's antiques shop, which wasn't even all that long ago, the automatons used to gather every few days in an enormous hall, each of them occupying their own little stage. The lights would come up and their motionless bodies, frozen by the magician's spell, would come back to life. The sword-swallower swallowed his sword, then spat it out, then swallowed it again; the devil mischievously removed his head and put it back, removed his head and put it back; the angel turned her face from the darkness to the light, from the darkness to the light, the light a bulb made to look like the sun. Their willpower seemed infinite. They were giving everything they had to the exact same series of motions, over and over again: the mechanical dog always barked the same way, and when it barked the mechanical horse always stopped its whinnying. It was only when the last guest had trickled away that their limbs and heads would gradually slow, and their voices would start to fade.

Did this mean the God whose Love moved them was the magician? In the church, whose love was moving Aliss? Owlish had said to her, 'Hold my hand and don't let go!' And then, as he shook off her hand, 'I love you. I love you.' Everyone had left the lift and she watched the chilly metallic doors slide neatly back together. Some kind of energy must have vanished behind them, because after that she could no longer move.

Wasn't the wooden Jesus nailed to the cross also God? Could he move her?

Aliss felt a great surge of energy rise in her body, deeper and more painful than any she had experienced before. God was surely within her, because now she could move her hands enough to push the music box lid fully open and then her legs enough to shuffle over to Jesus. She reached out to touch the back of his foot, then trailed her fingers over his toes. His toes, she noted, had been carved from dead trees, and the looping grain lines were full of tiny insects, like wriggling grains of rice, which crawled along the lines as if they were pathways. Were the insects God? What were they moving? She looked up at Jesus's drooping face, its surface as rucked and unsettled as the earth itself. She saw his face, and the shadow between his brows, and his wide, soundless mouth.

She wanted to help him, but she couldn't find a mechanism anywhere on his body. All she could do was embrace him. Well, except he was much higher up than she was, nailed up there on his cross, and so she only managed to embrace his feet. Love could move things, and she was convinced that her cold, stiff Jesus was starting to warm up. Not only that: he seemed to be shifting backwards. She let go of his feet and took a step away, which was when she noticed the seam in the wall behind him.

27

It was not yet night-time, but Nevers had already been taken over, once again, by blinding artificial lights. Professor Q hurried through the narrow streets, squeezing past other pedestrians, jostling their shoulders, leaving a trail of outraged glares in his wake. He had eyes only for the point behind them, above their heads, where the light was coming from. The light was so hot he felt as if his whole body was on fire. Two police officers appeared in the distance, walking side by side, heading in his direction. He looked around and discovered the street had emptied; there was only him and a row of cotton trees left, the fluffy cotton flower debris drifting in the air like ash. He turned and fled. Was someone yelling at him? He ran even faster, into a tunnel, where a man was camped out on a sleeping pad. Was this guy following him? The man was smirking. A string of shiny drink cans dangled from his body, rattling when he moved. At the end of the tunnel, a main road awaited. Cars raced past with their headlights on full beam, followed by a thundering double-decker bus that only narrowly avoided the pavement.

His legs went weak and his pace slowed. He wandered about, seemingly at random, but eventually found himself back in his own little neighbourhood where a sign on the fence around his housing estate caught his eye. PRIVATE PROPERTY NO UNAUTHORIZED ENTRY. The same sign appeared on all sides of the fence, its lettering bold and black. He wouldn't usually have paid it much attention, but on this particular day it felt comforting, authoritative, as though it was really there to protect him. Then he noticed a patrolling security guard and felt less convinced. He wasn't carrying his homeowner ID and the guard looked unfamiliar. Would the guard recognize him as a resident? It was just a little thing, but it threw him into a panic. His breathing grew laboured. Luckily, his block was nearby and the management office was right there at its entrance; to his relief, the supervisor's head was visible through the window. The automatic entrance doors parted, but when he passed the management office the supervisor's head didn't move, only his eyes. Why was the man looking at him like that? He didn't slow down to ask. In fact, he started running again.

What a relief to be back in his own home! Without turning on the light, he staggered inside, groping his way to somewhere near the sofa, where he collapsed on the floor. He was a mess, a string of junk only barely holding it together; he clutched his knees to his chest, trying to make himself as small as he possibly could. He felt like crying but his eyes remained stubbornly dry. His crotch, on the other hand, grew damp. No need to worry, he thought, accidents happened. He was pleased to realize how little shame he felt. He didn't even feel the urge to get up and change his clothes. No one else was home anyway. Or were they? Suddenly, he wasn't quite so sure.

Would a security camera be able to see through the dark to the wetness in his trousers? But, at his age, this was only normal. Surely even Owlish was caught out from time to time? He giggled. How strange that Owlish made no attempt to contradict him!

'Hey, buddy,' he called out, 'hast thou completely forsaken me?'

There was no response. He had given up on receiving any more help from Owlish, but still the silence was disheartening. Apparently, Owlish was not his buddy after all. In the beginning, hadn't he been in full support of the affair? And now that all hell had broken loose, he had vanished.

Owlish was really and truly his only friend, despite all those long years in Nevers. He had no one else to turn to. Now that he thought of it, when exactly had he first met Owlish? He tried to summon his friend's face, and Owlish's head turned slowly towards him in the darkness, its features much blurrier than before. Owlish laughed, the sound high-pitched and cunning, like the laugh of a teenage boy. Professor Q pressed his hands over his ears. He didn't want to hear it. Not because he envied Owlish; certainly not. Why should he? He had a respectable job, a high-ranking civil servant for a wife, a flat most people couldn't even dream of being able to afford. Knowing what Owlish was like, he was probably still drifting from place to place, no fixed employment, never quite knowing where his next meal was coming from.

Owlish might once have been his best friend, but that was years ago. The Owlish of today was surely very different to the Owlish of back then. Otherwise, there would be none of this funny business! It wouldn't be so hard to make head or tail of what he was saying. Owlish was a free spirit, a diehard layabout—why had he ever imagined that Owlish could understand what he was going through? And why, after so many years of absence, had Owlish reappeared in his life? Not to help him, that much was clear. Perhaps it all came down to jealousy on Owlish's part. Who was to say that Owlish hadn't sent that painting to his office in an attempt to frame him?

If he lost his job, he would lose everything. Pretty soon, news would get out about the university's accusations against him, in relation to both the painting and to Aliss. How was he supposed to explain any of this to Maria? Maria! Belatedly, Professor Q remembered his wife. She was on business in City H, but wasn't she due back today? He couldn't imagine how furious she would be if she were to learn how recklessly he had been behaving. And those ridiculous letters he had drafted, with all their broken sentences! Thinking of them now, the words hit his heart like icy bullets. Why on earth had he written any of them down? What had possessed him to think he wanted to leave his wife—his wife whom everyone loved and admired!—and run off with a doll? It was a path of absolute stupidity, and everyone he had ever known would turn their back on him if he followed it. He would be kicked out of his home, and the stable Nevers life he had built for himself would collapse like a line of dominoes. Maria could never see those letters. Luckily, his idiocy had not gone far enough for him to have actually sent them. There was still time.

He knew he should go and change out of his soaked trousers to avoid Maria coming home and seeing the state he was in, but he didn't. He was happy. For the time being, the flat and its mercifully thick, forgiving darkness was his and his alone.

28

Earlier that same day, the ringing of the telephone had shot through the quiet of the apartment like a bolt of lightning, rousing Maria from her stupor.

Mrs C's voice came on the line. It was not immediately clear what she was talking about, but Maria gradually realized it had something to do with a mistake she had made during the turmoil of the day before. She had no recollection of what that mistake was, nor why it required such an urgent gathering of her and the other ladies to 'have a little chat about it'. Still, she confirmed her presence at four o'clock that afternoon, assuring Mrs C that of course she would be there, no question about it.

She hung up the phone in a state of high anxiety. She had to pull herself together! Even if she had managed not to say anything during the call, her agitated tone of voice would have given Mrs C all sorts of clues. No matter what happened at this gathering, there was absolutely no way she could admit to her girlfriends that her husband was in love with another woman. Not even another woman! A foreigner *doll*.

She chose a well-ironed skirt suit from the collection in her wardrobe, hanging it over the front of the wardrobe door while she went into the bathroom. She had been wearing the same clothes for two days straight, and it was almost a shock to peel them off and see her creamy white breasts and still-firm torso in the bathroom mirror. The woman in the reflection didn't look half a century old. She was undeniably attractive—seductive, even. Maria was alarmed by the thought. She turned away and stepped into the tub. Soon after, the showerhead hissed and the mirror clouded over. Her thoughts returned to her husband in the church, weeping over his blonde doll. She was back to being her usual, reasonable self. Why had she been so quick to cast blame? He must be having some sort of breakdown. Was it the pressure of his job? Or was he reading too much? Whatever the cause, he was clearly in need of help, not accusations. Yes, the fact of the matter was: her husband needed her. Having thus found her way back to a sense of reality, she started to think that perhaps the impending ladies' get-together wasn't such a bad idea after all; it would help her shake off the last vestiges of this unnecessarily bleak mood.

As she was leaving her flat, Maria noticed the door of the flat opposite was slightly ajar. Through the crack, she spied a familiar childish face. A balm for her spirits!

'Hello, you,' she said. 'Would you like some candy?'

Carefully arranging her face into a smile, she rummaged in her handbag, looking for a treat to give the boy. Usually, she kept her bag stocked with fruit candies and red envelopes of pocket money, but on this occasion she came up short. The only thing she could dredge up, from right at the bottom of the bag, was a very old, clumsily made knot, squashed out of shape by all the items above it. A little embarrassed, she took it out and started to crouch down to eye level with the boy, but as she did so he slammed the door closed, sending an icy blast of air right into her face. She had time to notice that he'd been looking at her strangely, and she suddenly remembered seeing him in the hallway that morning, on her mad dash to the hotel. He would have seen her with her hair all messy, her eyes bloodshot . . . She must have looked a fright.

She stood back up, weighed down by a powerful sense of defeat. Her fighting spirit of just a few moments earlier seemed to have vanished. While things were still hidden, they weren't real. But once they came to light they settled like dust motes, and their previous non-existence was irrelevant; they became immutable facts. The child had seen her that morning, and no doubt could not stop thinking about how crazy she had looked. He might even have told his little friends about the scary lady from the flat opposite. Worse, he might have told his mother—

But now was not the time to think about it. She had this gathering to get through first. They were probably all there already, enthusiastically planning their approach. How much did Maria already know? How best to comfort her? What could they do to help? To think that something like this could happen *even with a husband like hers*.

Maria had left the housing estate and was almost at the subway station when she changed her mind, turned around, and headed for the supermarket in a nearby shopping mall. It was a supermarket chain found all over Nevers, well known for selling expired food, but it had been revamped for her nice, middle-class neighbourhood— given an elegant new name, wider aisles, and better lighting to showcase the colourful array of produce it imported from the other side of the world. Maria knew the store layout well, and quickly filled her basket with two bottles of red wine, a bottle of champagne, a platter of ham, and a box of lustrous imported strawberries. Striding out of the shop, weighed down with these purchases, she felt calm and purposeful.

When she arrived at Mrs C's house, the assembled women looked at her cautiously, steeling themselves to speak. Maria took a deep breath, her smile at the ready, her script already decided, and before any of them could open their mouths she announced: 'My, what a lovely day! It's been so long since we had sunshine like this!'

The women exchanged glances. There was a small pause, then one of them said: 'Mrs C tells us that—'

'What?' Maria glanced at Mrs C. 'Look, whatever silly thing I said—yesterday I was on a business trip and I got a little carried away, had a glass of wine too many, and as you know I'm not much of a drinker . . .

'But, seeing as we're here, there is something I want to talk about. You could say it's important, but on the other hand it's really nothing. It's just that lately I've been thinking we shouldn't let our husbands—shouldn't let *men*—become our whole worlds. We shouldn't need a reason to get together as just us girls! Don't you agree? Let's celebrate ourselves, for no reason at all!'

Maria looked at each of the women in turn, portioning out her smile like slices of birthday cake.

For a moment, the women sat in stunned silence. They had been storing up compassion and understanding, ready to be shoulders for Maria to cry on, and after all that her speech was something of a let-down. At the same time, they could breathe sighs of relief. Clearly Mrs C had been mistaken, everything was fine between Maria and her husband, their marriage as exemplary as always. The women were more than willing to believe it. A few of them stood up and began helping Maria take her shopping out of its plastic carrier bags, arranging the items on Mrs C's dining table.

'Look what treats Maria's brought us!' said one woman, unwinding the tiny cage from the top of the champagne.

The pop of the cork broke through the stuffiness of the afternoon, followed by a fountain of glistening bubbles. Someone turned on the radio, and the classical music channel broadcast an anonymous, sophisticated tune.

The women seemed to have started talking about something else. Maria was not really listening. She took a glass of champagne and looked off towards the small rectangular mirror inset in Mrs C's display cabinet, in which her reflected complexion looked porcelain-smooth. Despite the summer weather, her blouse was buttoned right up to her neck. Her face really did look impeccable, like a china ornament in a luxury exhibition. Her tears had dried, leaving behind no discernible trace. She sipped at her champagne and smiled at the person in the mirror—a practised smile, even more elegant than the classical music playing in the background.

29

A door swings open.

You reach through to the other side, feeling exhilarated, nervous, as if you're plunging your hand into a goodie bag of mysterious prizes. Your body follows your hand, tilts, and you see a ladder unfurled beneath you like a steely tongue. Somewhere in the distance water drips.

You climb down the ladder until your feet hit solid ground. The sound of water is clearer now, more of a rushing than a drip, and here by your feet is a filthy stream. Discarded objects clutter its surface and the stink is overpowering, but it indicates the way ahead. You hear a sound unlike any you have heard before and look up as a swarm of golden cockroaches flies past, wings glistening. Meanwhile, something greyish-green and enormous lurks in the water, drifting slowly with the current—a dead crocodile—and when you reach down to touch it, its skin is creased like cooled lava.

Paths and streams spread through this underground world, splitting like tree branches. A fork in a path is a good thing: it means you have to make a choice. And whichever direction you choose, you will have to abandon a part of yourself. You cannot remember, have been slowly forgetting, all the paths you have given up and all the parts of yourself you have had to abandon. Those given-up selves are still out there, continuing down all those given-up paths.

You walk through a doorway, you exit a doorway, you head for the light, you turn your back on the light. You see half-opened metal shutters, broken glass, steps leading who knows where. You ascend, you descend, everything in slow motion. On the horizon you see buildings, you see a city, you see civilization. Is this Nevers? If so, why do all the buildings look so decrepit, as though their skin has been peeled away, exposing the raw musculature beneath? You see blood-red graffiti daubed across walls: eyeballs bulging out of faces, machine guns protruding from a big, round belly and aiming directly at you.

You walk into a building and discover the building is actually an extension of another building. No, not an extension, not a building attached to another building, but a merging of buildings, many buildings folded and tangled together to form a huge architectural conglomeration. You see a machine like a hulking dead animal, its epidermis flaking and dark red with rust, its structure eaten away by shadows and dark green parasites. Somehow, you're back outside the building, standing on a steep road with no cars. Potholes in the road's surface have been filled with mud, from which sprout leaves like snake plant leaves, with the same vivid streaks. A dog scurries past, but when it glances back at you it has a human face. You think you hear birdsong, but when you look into the trees you see a long-haired man sitting on a branch, strumming an enormous comb. Then he opens his throat wide and he looks just like a bird, readying to fly away.

You meet a man calling himself a magician, dressed in a cloak and top hat.

'As a side effect of my medication, there's not a single hair left on my body,' he explains, bringing his face right up to yours, peering up at you from beneath lashless eyelids.

'Look! My eye colour is fading, soon I'll be completely transparent. If not for this cloak and hat, no one would see me at all!'

You notice that his cloak is actually a dark green canvas awning (the name of a fruit stand is written across it) and that his hat is made of old newspapers, what was once news now refashioned into decoration for his head.

You continue walking and discover, not far away, a girl dressed as a ballerina. Her feet are pressed together at the heel and pointing away from each other at the toe, and her hands are laced in front of her waist, her arms in a seemingly perfect circle. She is wearing a magnificent swan headdress just like one you own. You almost mistake her for yourself, except she's dressed in midnight black and standing on a cheap, mass-produced wooden box. In most other respects, she seems to be copying you. She has smothered her face in white paint, layers and layers of it, smoothing out any fine downy hairs, filling in all her pores, smothering the skin. Her lips have been smeared with a metallic tint while yours are rosy, because your creator based you on a human, trying desperately to give you life. You notice a card to the side of her box featuring several different kinds of script. You recognize the Valerian, which says: Mechanical Dream People.

It's as if you are back in the antiques shop. You see now that the girl is surrounded by other boxes, a frozen 'doll' standing on top of each one. Some of them are dressed in metal visors and full suits of armour, like Roman soldiers, their spears at the ready; others are in wizard robes wearing false pointy chins, their arms thrown wide as if casting spells. But you know they're not real dolls, despite their efforts to disguise themselves with costumes, make-up, those thick layers of paint to mask their skin's breathing. You see past it all to the faint trembling in their fingers and calves, the occasional careless blink, the one who looks on the verge of a sneeze—

You don't understand. Why are these living, breathing human beings pretending to be lifeless dolls? You notice the ballerina's box has no handle to wind it up. Instead, there's a picture of a coin with a queen's head on it, and beside the coin an arrow, pointing to a narrow opening. You scour the floor until your gaze lands on a crack in the concrete in which something shiny is catching the light. You walk over and find that, yes, it's a coin with a queen's head on it. You insert the coin into the slot in the box, something chimes, and one of the ballerina's arms moves from her waist to over her head, then one of her legs rises, bending to make a sixty-degree angle at the knee.

Then she freezes again. You wish you could insert more coins and make her continue, but you can't find any. You stand in front of her and stroke the black tights over her thigh. You find a hole and poke your finger through it. Her nostrils flare and the corners of her mouth twitch, then you hear a peal of laughter and her body seems to unclench. She sits down on the box and starts rooting around under her tutu, and from somewhere between the hole in her tights and a blood stain now visible on her thigh, she produces a lighter and cigarette. She hunches over to light up, takes a long drag, slowly exhales. She offers you the cigarette.

You accept, trying to copy her actions. You feel a warm current enter your body, but your body itself doesn't seem to change. Then the girl looks at you in alarm and yells, 'Hey! Your eyes are smoking!'

You don't know it, but she's speaking the local Nevers language. You don't understand a word but you see her start to laugh again, and then you're laughing too. It comes as a shock: you've never laughed like this before. The two of you sit laughing together on top of her box.

'What is this place?' you ask in Valerian. 'Is this Nevers?'

'So you're new here?' she says, switching to Valerian in response. 'Of course this is Nevers, just not completely. You could call it a shadow of Nevers—its subconscious, or maybe its dream. It's why we came.'

You ask if she didn't like wherever it was that she lived before.

She says, 'I liked it and I didn't like it. It's hard to explain. For example, I want to stay alive but I don't want to be human.'

You ask if it's better to be human or a human doll.

'Oh, we're not dolls. We're mechanical dream people.'

You say that you don't know what that is and she refuses to believe you.

'Dreaming allows us to transcend the bounds of reality, to fortify ourselves, to become as strong as machines. Look at us, we've been up on these boxes holding these positions for hours. Ordinary humans can't do that.'

You don't understand. Wouldn't it be better for them just to move freely, whenever they felt like it?

'Hard to say if that would be freedom or not. To be able to move is one kind of freedom, to be able to not move is another. I always thought I was a human, but after I got here I started to wonder. Who's to say I'm not a seahorse able to think like a human, or a wardrobe forced to smile and nod all day?'

The girl crooks a finger and taps it against her head.

'Who knows, maybe everything I've been up till now was just a programme someone implanted in my skull.'

'What about you?' she continues. 'Who are you?'

You tell her your name.

'Elise as in Beethoven's "Für Elise" or Alice as in *Through the Looking Glass*?'

Before you can answer, something chimes again. Someone has dropped a coin into her box, and she has to get back up. She raises both hands above her head this time and stretches her raised leg even higher, angling her body forward like a missile about to launch.

You leave her and the other dolls nearby, heading for a line of women styled like cleaning staff who have appeared in mid-air. Each one holds a long broom horizontally across her chest and is walking along a steel tightrope. Then, out of nowhere, you see a worker in a hard hat plunge from a crane—you cry out, only to see his face swing through the air like a pendulum, his mouth in a weary smile, his body held securely upside down by a rope tied around his ankle.

'This city contains dangers you can't even imagine, hundreds of thousands of them, lurking like bear traps in a wood.'

You turn to find a young woman. She is in a corner sitting next to a little girl, one hand gripping the girl's waist, the other a gleaming knife. The knife hovers above the girl's extended arm. You cannot believe how gentle the woman looks, how warm she is towards the girl, as if all she's doing is slicing a cake. The girl's arm is covered in knife wounds.

You ask if they, too, are mechanical dream people?

The little girl smiles.

'I'm about to start kindergarten,' she says. 'My mother is stepping up my training in how not to feel pain. One day, blood will no longer flow from my wounds.'

You snatch the knife from the woman's hand and stare dubiously at the light glinting off the blade. You look down at your own pale arm and take aim—

Professor Q opened his eyes to find himself in his own bed, the edge of the quilt soft and familiar against his cheeks. He felt as if he was waking from an extended dream, and for a moment the idea was a comforting one: it would all be over now. But his bones were in agony, creaking loudly with every tiny motion, to the point that he cried out for Maria. His head was burning! She had to come quickly and put the fire out!

Maria rushed into the bedroom, already dressed for work, and pressed a hand to her husband's forehead. Rather than being worried, she breathed a sigh of relief. At least he knew he was sick.

Her calm expression seemed to soothe him. He stopped thrashing around and lay still in the bed, trusting she would find a way to help. But before she could finish putting together an ice pack to cool the flames, the plaintive cry of the doorbell echoed through the flat.

'Two postmen are outside with a letter for you,' reported Maria, poking her head back through the bedroom door. 'It seems important. They need you to go and sign for it in person.'

Her tone was gentle, but the words sounded to Professor Q like an order, stabbing him in the back. Why was his wife trying to force him to interact with strangers?

'Tell them I'm unwell and not receiving post today.'

Maria left again, only to return a few minutes later.

'Apparently I was mistaken. They're not postmen, they're just wearing the same uniform as the postman. I'm not sure which department they're from, but they have official badges and say you have to go with them. I think you'd better freshen up and get going.'

Professor Q remained in bed, pulling the sheets tighter around him.

'If you don't get up by yourself, they'll come in here and do it for you.'

'No, don't let them in!' yelled the professor, his voice bordering on a roar. Then a note of resignation crept in.

'Fine,' he added, more quietly. 'If that's how it is, give me a minute to get dressed and I'll be there.'

If there were really a fire inside his skull, burning through all the useless garbage, shouldn't his head be getting lighter? Instead it felt impossibly heavy. This heaviness, combined with the raging fever, led him to a point of outright despair. But despair wasn't such a bad feeling, because while he was despairing he was no longer afraid. Those two postmen could hardly make things worse.

They were waiting for him outside the front door, just as Maria had said. To show his contempt, the professor refused to meet their eyes as they led him down the building hallway; he kept his head down and focused on their green trouser cuffs and shiny leather shoes. As he passed the entrance to the flat opposite, he caught a brief glimpse of the little boy, who was crouched behind the security grille and staring at him wide-eyed, grinning in apparent delight.

To Professor Q's horror, the two postmen characters escorted him to a minivan exactly like the one he had used with Aliss. They hopped in the driver's compartment, leaving him alone in the back. There was nothing there: no sound system, no fridge, no sofa, just a cold hard bench that hurt to sit on. The fire inside his head continued to rage, despite the van's freezing temperature. He looked down at his feet and observed, regretfully, that the trousers he'd chosen were much too lightweight. His one shred of comfort came from the windows, which were still one-way glass, meaning nobody could peer in and see him.

Had he been arrested? They hadn't put him in handcuffs, and no one was sitting back there guarding him. Maybe the situation wasn't as serious as it seemed?

The van headed north. He had assumed it would take him to the university, but it drove right past the turn-off. The high-rise buildings started to thin out until eventually there were none at all, and the van turned onto a bumpy lane. A sparkling fish pond emerged from behind a line of trees, egrets swooping across the water, followed by an expanse of green lawn, then a small hill. The hill was surrounded by a stone wall behind which he could see the tops of sloping, European-style tiled roofs.

The postmen let him out of the van and marched him to a high-security metal gate in the wall. CCTV cameras had been mounted on top of it, and a palm-sized electronic sensor was positioned to one side. The postmen tapped electronic passes lightly against the sensor, and the gate automatically opened. The space enclosed by the walls was even larger than the professor had imagined: the three of them had to walk across another enormous stretch of lawn to reach one of the sloping-roofed buildings. From the outside, the building looked sturdy, high quality, the style that of a European cottage; standing there looking at it, bathed in warm sunlight, Professor Q felt almost as though he were on holiday.

Once he stepped into its gloomy interior, however, he started to feel nervous. The front door closed behind him, making it almost impossible to see. Someone guided him to a seat. After a while his eyes adjusted, and he realized he was sitting at one end of a long rectangular table that stretched away from him to a distant point deep inside the room. At the far end, he could make out a number of burly male figures, some of them sitting, others standing up. None

189

of them were in uniform but their taut, impassive faces conveyed the same intimidating effect as uniforms would have done. A thick black curtain had been pulled across the floor-to-ceiling window behind them, blocking any view of the scenery outside.

A beam of projector light forced Professor Q to screw his eyes shut. When he opened them again, a large screen was slowly descending behind the men. It showed a multicoloured map of Nevers—but, wait, had something happened to his eyesight? Beneath the lines of the slightly off-centre map, he saw a duplicate line. No, not one, but many! Duplicate lines, shadow images: hidden beneath the city was a whole a cluster of ghostly cities.

'Does this seem strange to you?' asked the man at the centre of the group. 'The maps we're all used to seeing are even stranger. How on earth could a single printed map be expected to capture a world as deep and complex as the one we inhabit?'

Noting poor Professor Q's uncomprehending expression, the man smiled and signalled for an assistant to change the slide. A landscape photo appeared, showing a big blue ocean and a small green island. A reassuringly normal image, until the assistant brought up shots taken from different angles and Professor Q felt himself break out in a cold sweat. How could he have been so slow? It was Aliss's island! That was his church!

But if they knew about Aliss, it was hardly surprising they had found out about the church. Surely they couldn't put him in jail for occupying an abandoned church? Adultery was not a criminal offence!

'Don't worry,' said the man in the centre, as though reading his thoughts. 'We're delighted you borrowed the church. Otherwise we might never have noticed its value as a strategic location from which to launch an attack against the shadow zone.

'What's that, Professor? Have you not heard of the shadow zone?

'Did you not wonder where all the students went? The ones who didn't return to university after the strike? They weren't at home.

And without supplies or shelter, how was their revolution to stand a chance of success?'

At the words 'strike' and 'revolution', the fire in Professor Q's brain intensified. He could hear the chattering of his own teeth.

'The students who fled your class are all there, you know. The shadow zone is the student rebel headquarters. Now we need to take a good look around your church to see if we can use it as a base.'

'You're saying you want to use the church as the base for a crackdown?'

'Professor Q, be mindful of your words! We are only taking the necessary measures to restore social order.'

'But what help am I in all this?'

'Why don't we turn that question around? I'm more interested in what *we* can do to help *you*. You've been active on the island for quite some time. The best thing would be if you would take us there and show us around, especially if that involved an on-site investigation of the church. That would be ideal. We are perfectly capable of going by ourselves, but we're keen to maintain good relations with the university, and to expand our friendship circle. Hence we're willing to offer you the chance to explain yourself. That is, the chance to make it quite clear that you had nothing to do with the student uprising.'

'If this is the case, could I first go to the church and tidy up a bit, perhaps dispose of any personal items?'

The man roared with laughter.

'Professor Q, there's no time for that! We were hoping you would take us right away. I'm a married man too, you know. Sometimes I also like to dream, it helps balance out the dullness of real life. But what happens in a dream stays in a dream. It doesn't affect reality. We're here now, and this is your chance to destroy those dreams of yours, along with any incriminating evidence of them.'

31

A light flits across your face. Or maybe it doesn't. The only thing you know for sure is that you're on Valeria Island, in a high-end café on the ground floor of a shopping mall. You and your girl-friends have been sitting on the café's soft, dreamy-hued sofas for hours. Each piece of cutlery has been polished to an immaculate silver gleam, and the floor-to-ceiling windows are crystalline from the dutiful ministrations of the sun. You look idly at the view out-side. A railing worms along the seafront, and behind it people stand in small clusters, blurred by the sunset into impressionist smudges against the horizon. A tour guide wields a travel agency flag like a conductor's baton, ushering his charges into the mall. Further off, beneath five towering flagpoles whose flags you can't make out, a street performer flings his arms wide and shrugs a basketball across his shoulders. People smile at him as they walk by. A few even pause and let handfuls of coins clatter into his tip jar.

Sounds are fading out. Now you're uncertain of everything you thought you saw, because everyone on the promenade has gone. A cloud of sickly brown smoke rises in the distance, and from it emerges a line of green-black creatures with bionic compound eyes and pro-truding insect mouths, but with bodies that are stiff and human-shaped. They're marching in your direction. You know your friends are waiting for you to make some witty remark, but the fly-men have taken over your thoughts. Are they some kind of mutant? Except, in an international city like this one, wouldn't the ministry of health have issued a warning? You scream for everyone to look at the flies. You scream, The flies are coming for us! But as soon as the words leave your mouth they seem ridiculous even to you, impossibly so, and the invisible machinery of the café muzak works its magic, distorting and transforming your words, sucking out any trace of your voice, making sure nobody hears a thing.

You look around the café, at all those soft faces bathed in honeyed light, at the flickering shadows. A pair of silver tongs appears beside you, meticulously placing a sugar-dusted strawberry at the centre of the whipped cream on top of a slice of cake. A waiter in white gloves brandishes a long-spouted stainless steel jug and a stream of hot water arcs preposterously through the air, landing in the coffee filter on the table below. You pick up the ornately painted cup and saucer in front of you and they tremble in your hand. The porcelain clinks. You turn back to the window. There's no mistaking it: in one hand the fly-men hold black truncheons; in the other, shields. They are banging the truncheons against the shields.

The smoke is getting thicker, and people are scurrying out from within it. They're wearing flip-flops and house clothes—undershirts, shorts—and some are carrying spoons and wok lids. One of them pounces athletically with a fish steamer, extinguishing a tiny plume of smoke. Some girls in pink tutus race past the café window, their hair scraped into buns, presumably part of a summer dance school. One of them trips, falls to the ground, and is immediately surrounded by fly-men. A fly-man straddles her, the straps are torn off her leotard, her hair ribbon trembles, her reddened face turns to you. Something hard bashes relentlessly against her head and you see blood seep from her hairline. You start screaming, you scream to your friends, Look! The fly-men forced me to the ground! Then you realize you're being silly again. Your friends think it's hilarious. You glance at them, briefly wishing you could laugh like they're laughing, but your attention is on the window. You watch as blood spreads across the ground, the floor-to-ceiling window glass already stained red.

The fly-men are smacking their truncheons against the window, and the noise batters your eardrums. The glass is cracking! You keep your mouth closed and point frantically, hoping that now, at last, your friends will stop this insane charade. But a waiter sets down a slice of cake and instantly all the dainty dessert forks are covered in cream. There's no point saying anything anymore: the fly-men are inside the mall. People run in all directions, shopping bags in hand. Someone urges a shop assistant to hurry, to pack up their crystal swan figurine quickly, but a minute later the swan lies · smashed on the floor. Now the fly-men have reached the café and everyone is screaming. A fly-man approaches you, a shield on your back pins you to the ground. A voice says, What the hell are you doing here? The question strikes you as funny, you want to laugh, but somehow you seem to be sobbing. You say, I'm having afternoon tea! But you're on the floor, your voice a whimper, and nothing you say has any credibility at all.

The shield eases off your back and your mind clears. You yell, It's not me you're after, it's her! You try to point at the ballerina outside the window, but someone has twisted your arms behind your back and handcuffed you. They shout: Do not resist! You are obviously her! For the first time, you attempt to look around the café from this new perspective—so many shiny leather brogues and fashionable high heels, elegant even while running around in panic. The café carpet, you notice now, is exceedingly soft. You rub your face against it. You fantasize about nestling in it and falling fast asleep.

Isn't it Sunday? Just an ordinary Sunday, the one day of the week you can forget about work and let your thoughts drift. Has some new legislation just passed, outlawing daydreaming on Sundays?

Even on Sundays you feel guilty about not working. It's like that time you ran away from ballet class as a child, going to sit beside a fountain instead. The cool spray of water felt so good against your face, but mixed in with that pleasure was the dark shadow of wrong-doing. What if you actually are that girl outside? You're confused. Maybe you're not you, you're someone else.

They pass you a flimsy top and trouser set, the colour of ditchwater. It stinks like ditchwater too. You walk along a dark passage. They take away your name and assign you a five-digit number. Once you've changed into your new clothes, you enter an austere workshop filled with countless yous. Every you has her head bowed and is holding the kind of sign you see on streets everywhere: Do Not Enter. Do Not Run. Do Not Proceed. Do Not Retreat. Do Not Talk. Do Not Anything, Everything Is Forbidden. Every you has her head bowed and is silently manufacturing more of these prohibitions. Nobody has explained anything, but you know that even if all of you is not actually you, everyone here is you.

They bring their mouths to microphones and their voices balloon to fill the room. Get in line, they say. They whip out tape measures and measure the length of your skirts. Those found to be in viola-tion of the rules are slapped across the calves—or, wait, are they being groped? None of you make a sound. No wicked thoughts, the voices say. No chit-chat. Remain in position until you hear the bell.

You realize you're back at school. Time has come full circle, but your eyelids are so heavy. You try to catch someone's eye, someone like you, looking forward to breaktime when you can shriek and laugh and let your mouth spout whatever silly thoughts it likes. Inside the demarcated break area, you all sprint around without caring that if you're mid-sprint when the bell stops you'll have to freeze like that. Prohibitions are games to you. Someone ends up with a leg awkwardly outstretched, an uneaten biscuit poised in her wide-open mouth. You find one another hilarious, and when the prefects come by to inspect you, sporting their gold and scarlet armbands, it's very hard not to laugh. You pull a face at one, expecting her to crack a smile, but instead she brings her face close to yours and says she'll have to report you. And now you can hold it in no longer; you burst out laughing. The earnestness of her expression is too much!

You hear a whistle. You and all the other yous are on an exercise ground. Some of you are playing football, others walking around, others doing gymnastics. Some of you are gazing at the sky, watching clouds go by. Some of you have your eyes closed, as if focusing on the feeling of the air against your skin. You don't understand why you're here, playing the role of prisoner—when did breaktime finish? You no longer feel like laughing. You open your mouth as wide as it will go and attempt to exhale from deep in your chest, releasing air in raspy huffs. A guard springs to attention. You watch fear sweep across her rigid features. One hand moves to the truncheon at her waist, the other hand rises to her mouth, her cheeks expand, she's about to blow on her whistle—

You do as you are told, kneeling with your hands on your head. How did all this start? You try to remember. No, not because of the student arrests. Not because the government insisted on pushing through a cross-border bridge construction project that ran severely over budget. Not because the seaside sitting-out areas were turned into army barracks. Not because the history textbooks were altered and your memory warped. Not because a member of the opposition party was forbidden to run for election. Not because police bullets made protesters' eyes bleed down their faces. Not because of manhunts inside public hospitals. Not because people are arrested and then three days later discovered with all their bones broken. Not because yet another hopeless protester has thrown themselves off a roof. Not because the police switchboard operator says, 'You'd better be afraid—'

You close your eyes. You know everything has to start somewhere. You should have seen this coming.

You pick one of your old university notebooks out of a pile of junk. The first few pages are filled with neatly written lecture notes but then the writing abruptly stops. A number of pictures have been stashed between two of the blank pages that come after—

You think back to a long-ago Wednesday afternoon, Room 000 of some university lecture block. You're always there for something, and this time it's Introduction to Literature, a required class. The content is abstract, boring, and although ostensibly you and every other student in the room are calmly seated, your minds wander like restless ghosts. Smartphones barely exist yet and you're all slumped over your desks taking notes by hand, earnestly trying to grasp the essence of the professor's meandering sentences. But when you turn your attention from what the professor is saying to his drooping eyelids and the vacant eyes beneath, you realize this isn't really him. The unfashionable suit, the tie pulled so tight that it's a miracle he can breathe at all—no, this is not his true form.

How could you have failed to see it before? He's rambling on and on, mumbling to himself; this is not the voice of a living human being. The same goes for all the half-dead students sitting dumbly in their seats, going through the motions of note-taking: it's all a pretence. The realization comes to you in a rush. You've been showing up here, week in, week out, always exactly on time, and it's a scam, it always has been: a collective ruse carried out by the professor and students, over and over again. The only goal is the illusion of glory for the university, an institution no longer capable of inspiring any meaningful new thought whatsoever.

The real professor has ventured boldly into a dream state, an act of rebellion against himself. His eyes swivel, transformed into coloured glass beads, and his eyebrows are rising up his forehead. He casts an enormous shadow onto the whiteboard behind him, and the shadow calls out to you. The professor solemnly requests that everyone turn to page fifteen of their textbooks, but what he is really saying is: *Surely you don't believe anything you read in textbooks?* When you notice people actually turning to page fifteen of their books, you have to clap a hand across your mouth to stifle your laughter.

The pretend professor continues to teach, while the squirming shadow pinned down by his feet—the real professor—rips off its suit and tie. The shadow is clearly getting impatient with the act: its hands and feet are pawing at the ground, and it's howling. It has a long muscular tail, waving in the air like a cat's, but the tufted head and hooked beak of an eagle owl. It leaps onto a desk, then vanishes through an open window. You get up to see where it's gone, but as you do everyone turns to look: all the students, the fake professor. You sit back down. As you sit there, trying to restrain yourself, you notice how many of your classmates have restless shadows. Their shadows are getting up and fleeing the lecture hall, one after another, congregating outside in the sun. You look at the floor and see that your shadow is struggling too, trying to wrest itself from your body. When it finally breaks free it doesn't rush outside, it heads for the teaching platform. Up there beneath the podium lights, retaining your exact outline, it grows to immense proportions. Then it begins to strip. As the outer layer of clothes come off, you see the gentle swell of breasts, the curve of a waist, and a skirt fanned out like a broken umbrella. It's a tutu, and beneath the tutu appears the outline of two strong legs. The legs are shadows, but there's no mistaking their strength—that kind of musculature takes years of training.

You took ballet as a child but could never get the positions right. The teacher was always throwing things at you. Eventually you got so angry that you stormed out of class, declaring you would rather die than step foot there again. You have no idea when your shadow would have snuck back in to practise.

Now, your shadow's feet curve out into crescent moons, then one rises, the toe touching the opposite knee, all the weight shifting to one side. The pose looks like one you've seen before, only this time there's nothing elegant about it. The shadow starts to spin. It's a classic pirouette, except the spinning is happening so fast that the toe on the floor is like the head of an electric drill, boring to unfathomable depths. When the pirouette ends, the thud of the shadow's ensuing dance steps make your notebook and pens jump about on your desk with incredible, machine-like force.

Your classmates continue to stare blankly ahead. You can't tell if they're seeing the shadow too. The shadow slows down and peels off what turns out to have been a wig, revealing a smooth scalp beneath, the hair cropped close like a soldier's. Next it removes its tutu and bodice, releasing a pair of pendulous breasts. There's a tiny *thing* between its thighs, and you watch in alarm as this thing grows into something resembling a long tail, which shoots across the platform. The shadow begins to talk, using your voice to speak coquettishly to the professor.

'Want a little feel?'

Now you understand why the shadow has stayed inside the lecture room: it intends to destroy every last bit of order. You are feverish with excitement, although beneath your excitement lurks a creeping embarrassment. The professor's eyebrows are raised; otherwise his face is perfectly expressionless. He is ignoring the shadow but other people are not, and you're afraid they will know you're responsible. You close your eyes. Everything is clearer when viewed from behind closed eyes.

All the other students have left, and the professor is packing up his briefcase. You both have shadows cowering beneath your feet. Is this it for the dream-state adventure? The professor's eyelids look leaden, and his arms and legs are tucked away inside his bad suit. You get up from your seat and catch up with him as he leaves, walking by his side. His footsteps quicken, and therefore yours do too. You turn to face him, give him a wink, and discover he is sound asleep. His closed eyes feel like an insult. He will not acknowledge what has happened, and you refuse to accept his refusal. You whirl around; your shadow follows.

You and your shadow will chase those memories of yours and pin them down in paint. Painting will reveal to you everything that time has concealed. A long-gone dream reaches out and grabs you by the throat: you remember the professor's name and look him up online. He's still teaching at the same university, and it's easy enough to find out his office address. You pull an envelope with the university insignia from your junk pile, and slip a painting inside.

32

Sunlight came to rest soundlessly on the backs of Professor Q's hands, nuzzling the skin and its blooming age spots like a warm-blooded animal. Professor Q looked down at the light and realized with a jolt that he must have been sitting in his empty study for hours. The warmth against his hands made him think of Aliss. Not all of her, but specifically her slightly parted lips, her fingers as they reached for him, her fingertips pressing into aching knots in his muscles. A vision of her began to materialize in the air before him, although no matter how hard he concentrated he could not conjure her eyes. Some minutes later, he felt a faint dampness in the crotch of his trousers; he reached down to touch it, then brought his fingers to his nose. Not urine, he could be thankful for that. It was a belated wet dream, a pathetic, barely there sprinkle of youth, over almost before it had begun.

'Here, drink this.'

When had Maria come in? She set down a porcelain cup with a fine-boned handle, filled to the brim with a steaming yellow liquid. What was it? Professor Q tried and failed to come up with an answer. He began to sip the drink, continuing until the cup was empty and an intense, bitter taste had taken over his mouth.

He looked at the emptiness around him, feeling as though his brain, too, had been scooped clean. What had he done all day? He dimly remembered going out for a stroll that morning. Yes, that was it: he had gone out to stretch his legs and been shocked to discover that a white enclosing wall had sprung up nearby his housing complex. The wall was very high and seemed to stretch infinitely into the distance. He had walked along it, passing twisty-limbed banyans, the holey, yellowing lawns of abandoned football pitches, art house cinemas with peeling film posters flapping sadly out front, a stray cat flashing through a makeshift junkyard—all these images were projected onto the wall, jostling for space, putting on a special performance just for him.

At a certain point he felt he had gone too far, but as he was deliberating whether to turn back, he noticed two workers in white coats wearing folded newspaper hats that looked like tiny upturned boats. The workers were touching up the paint on one section of the wall, but the section was pristine, already perfectly white; their ministrations were clearly superfluous. He had smiled approvingly. But, as he did so, a different scene appeared in his mind's eye: a mirror image of the wall, except that in this version it was splattered with foul-smelling urine and there was a row of detained persons crouching at its foot. They were silent, heads bowed, and resembled a heap of dark, beaten-down shadows.

'What are you up to here? When will the work be finished?'

'Our work here will never be done.'

The worker spoke in the voice of a middle-aged man but had a distinctively feminine face and an oddly tender smile, which gradually expanded, dispersing across those feminine features the way a drop of blood spreads through a pool of water. When the smile was over and the worker's expression had settled back into place, Professor Q had taken a good look at his (or her) eyes. They seemed congested, overly stuffed with messages they needed to convey, and as a result they were drooping and unfocused.

The professor felt a powerful urge to take out his notebook and jot something down, but before he could do so the other worker turned and said:

'Don't believe everything you see.'

This worker's face reminded him of a news reporter who had gone missing a few years earlier. The reporter had been on television reporting some big news story at the time of the disappearance. During the broadcast, Maria had been intently focused on tearing apart a honey-braised chicken leg. Professor Q had pointed at the events occurring on screen but found that his throat was too blocked with phlegm to get any words out. All he could do was gesture helplessly as colour leeched from the reporter's face, his complexion paling to that of a drowned corpse, the big news story sinking into the ocean along with it. The news reporter had turned his face away before Professor Q had had the chance to remember it properly.

'As soon as anything appears on the wall, we have to be here to paint over it. You get what I'm saying?'

He had watched as the workers bent down in unison, picked up the two paint cans sitting at their feet, and launched the contents at the wall. Thick white paint smacked onto the surface like a cresting wave, then ran along it, trickling down to the base and seeping across the ground towards where he was standing. He felt the disorder in his mind gradually smooth out, until all that was left was a perfectly flat white wall and the overpowering scent of toluene.

A rousing tune started up, and he began to tremble.

He turned around. Now the study door loomed before him like an enormous mouth, lips parted to barely a crack. The national anthem was blasting in from the living room, and would be followed by the news. His ears were pricked, he was listening, but all he heard was white noise. Then the flat was quiet again, and he decided to leave the study. In the living room, the television was turned off and Maria was sitting at the dining table, apparently sorting through some paperwork. When she saw Professor Q, she tucked the documents swiftly out of sight.

'Did something . . . I mean, what's the news today?'

Professor Q avoided Maria's eyes, trying to keep his voice from trembling.

'Nothing. Nothing happened.'

Professor Q went to sit on the sofa. All he could hear now was the pulsing of the second hand as it moved around the clock on the living room wall. It was a furtive, urgent sound, as though the clock were trying to communicate with him.

'Maria, do you remember a friend of mine called Owlish?'

Maria stared at him intently, as if an important coded message were written across his face.

'No,' she said, at last. Her gaze shifted slightly to one side, and she smiled. 'Never heard of him. You need to get your head out of the clouds. Didn't you say your tenure application has finally gone through? After all these years! We should do something tonight to celebrate.'

'Maybe some other night,' said Professor Q. 'I feel so tired.'

'You're much too stressed, that's your problem. I've made an appointment for you next week with David, we'll get you thoroughly checked out.'

David? Professor Q thought of those sky-blue pills he would no longer have any reason to take and almost felt like laughing. He knew there was nothing David could do to help him, but he didn't oppose his wife's suggestion. How could he? He was fast asleep, his upper body collapsed into the sofa. Maria came to stand over him, regarding his body as she might a placid lake. The sleeping pill had worked quickly, just as David had promised.

She went into the bedroom and unlocked her dressing table drawer, removing an old biscuit tin decorated with pictures of trees. The biscuits themselves were long gone, as was any trace of their smell; the tin now served as a repository for memorabilia. She poked through ancient letters, blurry ticket stubs, and a tangle of other such objects until she reached a slim, crudely bound volume of poetry, the word OWLISH printed across the front cover. Her husband had been through a phase of using it as a pen name. Without opening the book, she carried it into the kitchen and turned on the stove. The paper instantly caught fire. Sparks rose into the air and the book grew fiery wings, but she dumped it into a metal cleaning bucket before it could take flight. The paper cowered amid the flames, rapidly transforming into scorched black residue.

On her way through the living room, Maria looked out of the narrow window grille to the darkened bay beyond. Many of the dredgers were still illuminated, their immense mechanical arms twinkling as they rose slowly into the air. For a moment, her thoughts turned to the map in the misdirected email of a few months earlier, and she imagined one of those mechanical arms extending its iron palm and taking aim at her flat. She closed her eyes, readying herself to go down with it. But nothing happened, all was calm, and when she opened her eyes again the arm was plunged deep into the seabed.

When the dredger once again raised its single, twinkling limb high into the night, Maria thought it looked like a futuristic ballet dancer engaged in a slow pirouette. She smiled briefly, then remembered she still had a report to finish. Before getting back to work, she glanced at her sleeping husband. That business with his so-called mistress now seemed like a long-ago joke. His head looked like a wizened old apple, and to Maria the end-of-summer night felt like someone breathing into her ears, making her—at least for a single fleeting moment—full and whole once again.

Summer ends in an endless spool of barbed wire and countless pairs of narrowed, mistrusting eyes. The barbed wire and the military-patrolled road alongside it are from last century, laid to block unauthorized arrivals from inland Ksana. These days, despite numerous refurbishments and reinforcements, the border looks somehow feebler than before. This is especially true after sunset, when the bowed heads of the streetlights gaze peacefully down upon it, as though it were not even there.

Since the easing of immigration regulations between Nevers and inland Ksana, the border has been in a state of steady transformation, expanded by the assembling crowds into a whole new territory, belonging to neither side. During the day, smugglers take over the lanes with suitcases, foam coolers, cardboard boxes. Trains tear past every few minutes, several hundred of them a day, bringing with them the needle-fine shrieking of wheels against tracks. Waves of a putrid, sewage-like stink rise from the river beneath.

It smells like someone died, people whisper to one another, hands clamped over their noses.

In the sea around Nevers, and in the rivers that run through it, dead bodies have been floating to the surface. Such young corpses, their delicate, tofu-pale hands bound together with rope, the bloody wounds on their arms darkened to the colour of bruises. People pick them up and note the heaviness of their backpacks, which they open to find full of sodden bricks. But the bodies themselves are extraordinarily light, like human-shaped inflatable toys; a pinch and they might pop. Where do the bodies keep coming from? How many hidden caves does the city have, how many layers of underworld?

People go to the beach to make offerings to the gods, sending flurries of white rose petals sailing off into the creases of the ocean. White foam crawls up the sand in response, murmuring as if it has something to say. The corpses turn to ash. Fire after fire is lit. The cause of death is never suspicious. People think fleetingly of videos they've seen on the internet, there briefly then gone. Truncheons smacking down. Toppled bodies crushed beneath a knee, or a shield. Blood spilled in the deepest part of the night, and spreading. Where have the arrested people gone?

People dream of the sound of flesh torn from bone. There's a church, and a line of people kneeling before Jesus, hands cuffed behind their backs. Is that him—or her—looking up? Looking up with eyes like two deep wells, an inaudible sound trapped reverberating in their depths. Is Aliss among these people? If Aliss has been thrown into the sea and vanished beyond the horizon, will there be any trace of her among the floating corpses?

If, once all this is over, Aliss returns to the church—well, then the Jesus statue will still be there, up on the wall surveying the congregation, but aside from that everything will have changed. Professor Q's bookcases are already gone, along with all his books, the four-poster bed, the dressing table, the wardrobe, even the music box. Cardboard boxes and a few worn-out chairs lie strewn across the floor. If Aliss inadvertently steps on one of the abandoned takeaway boxes, flies will swarm out.

It can't really be, can it?

People continue to discuss the dead-person stench.

A banknote slides into a briefcase. Someone drags away their goods. What is inside the suitcases, foam coolers, cardboard boxes? Freshly extracted human organs, smuggled pork, counterfeit alcohol decanted into branded bottles, fake meat dumplings stuffed with garbage and ground-up paper. The border guards ask no questions. Their arms are folded. Beneath their expressionless faces lurks a kind of pleasure. The law is a silent plaster statue holding a set of scales, and they are its true enforcers. They could spring into action at any moment, or they could choose not to.

But now there's a commotion. People are crowding the riverbank, and two of the on-duty officers start to pay attention. People are hauling something out of the water. First they see long matted hair, then tattered clothing, then snow-white skin. Someone asks if the woman is dead. As she's lifted from the water, her eyelashes flutter. She's smiling. Her eyes open. Someone screams. Someone asks why her skin is so smooth. Shouldn't she be bloated from drowning? Someone is brave enough to touch her, and they realize she's a doll. Such a lifelike doll! Now everyone wants to touch her. Someone pokes a finger into one of her eyes, then dissolves into raucous laughter.

The two guards shrug at each other, grinning now, letting all their illicit memories sink back down where they belong. As they turn to walk back to their post, one brags to the other that even if the corpse had been real, they have their ways. They could still have thrown her out with the trash.

However, as they continue, backs straight, faces still smiling, something prevents them from feeling truly at ease. They come to a halt. The crowd was laughing a second ago, why is it screaming now? The guards whirl around to see everyone still clustered about the toy. The motionless body is face up on the ground, still dressed in that torn-up clothing through which fragments of flesh are visible, impossibly pale, impossibly lifelike. The guards can even see the fine webs of blood vessels beneath her skin, laid out like a mysterious map. One of her arms is thrown out to the side, and a bright red liquid is welling up from a fine slit in her arm—so vivid, so abundant, and it's surging now, coming on in an unquenchable torrent.

Afterword

念念不忘

Lingering in Mind

Perhaps we can describe a novel as an echo, or the response in a sequence of call and response. I sent out my call for this one many years ago, so many that I couldn't tell you anymore what exactly the call was. Now, a response has found its way back.

In the autumn of 2011, I brought a story with me to the University of Iowa's International Writing Program. I was staying in a downtown hotel with a ground-floor bar. The bar had an outdoor seating area strung with tiny lights, like Christmas tree decorations, and most evenings people were out there getting drunk. I could look down on them from my room, and it felt like looking at a dream, so close I could almost touch it. I was often drunk too, either in the cave-like confines of the Fox Head—a rickety tavern beloved by visiting writers—or in the Takanami sushi bar, where I went to drink sake with S. The mornings after, I would run into the Singaporean writer with the impeccable British accent and the right words for every occasion, and his ghost of a frown would stir up the shame my wiped-clean memory otherwise refused to let me access.

It was a sad period of my life. I often trudged along the Iowa City pavements fantasizing about throwing myself on the ground and never getting up again—not even if one of the city's surreal mounted horses happened to come past, a strapping young policeman on its back.

One evening S came to my room in a panic, saying she had lost her wallet. It turned out to be waiting for us at the police station, all its coins and banknotes magically lined up across a blank sheet of paper, displayed like museum exhibits. Since arriving in the United States, S had been sniffling all day long, wondering if she was allergic to something. She faded into background of our group of writers. But the night we found her wallet she came alive, shouting her joy through the empty streets, yelling that we had to celebrate with pizza.

S's voice echoing through the midnight city is one of my most cherished memories. This novel feels indebted to it, even if I couldn't tell you now what I actually wrote during my stay in Iowa—just as I couldn't tell you about any of those nights when I was drunk, acting my part in dreams with people I had only just met. Everything that happened during that time feels fragile, as if it barely existed, including the words I typed into my computer while holed up in my room above the bar. When I came back to Hong Kong, most of the files turned out to be corrupted and couldn't be restored, leaving me with only the title.

But that's not strictly true. The story of Owlish and Aliss had been with me since long before then. And, as far as I'm concerned, the novel was finished a long time ago too. It's just that it was hanging there, with nowhere to land. The political situation in Hong Kong has been changing by the day and this story has been in flux with it, as if the city itself were deciding the destiny of Owlish and Aliss.

During the 2014 Occupy Movement, protesters chanted with the fervour of church choirs, urging the city to *wake up*. In Cantonese it's one syllable—*sing*—neat and clear, ringing out like a decisive moral judgement. In 2019, almost two million people took to the streets. Was that because they had woken up? But more and more often you hear that protesters are 'dreaming'. Going to a demonstration no longer feels like heading out to a party with friends. With your face covered, sneaking into a city you thought you knew, are you still yourself? Or have you crossed to another world, where the streets are unpredictable and the people strangers, where you might at any moment run into some unknown dream version of yourself? I'm thinking of Walter Benjamin's obsession with the Parisian arcades. For him, they were a bygone world, a dreamscape divorced from reality, but precisely in that dialectic between dreaming and waking, at the point where the material world and one's innermost being meet, the past suddenly opens wide to the present and, for a split second—for a *ksana*, that Buddhist notion of the smallest possible moment—we attain the state of awakening.

Which is to say: if I see Owlish and Aliss in Hong Kong, it isn't because people here have finally awoken from a dream, but rather because the city exists at the intersection of dreaming and being awake. The past flashes up again and, in that instant, in that brief present-moment mirage, you feel yourself getting closer to the call— you've forgotten it but it's there, whispered, persistent, almost coming back.

1 June, 2020

DOROTHY TSE is the author of several short-story collections and has received the Hong Kong Book Prize, Hong Kong Biennial Award for Chinese Literature, and Taiwan's Unitas New Fiction Writers' Award. Her first book to appear in English, *Snow and Shadow* (translated by Nicky Harman), was longlisted for the Best Translated Book Award. She is the co-founder of the literary journal *Fleurs des Lettres*.

NATASCHA BRUCE translates fiction from Chinese. Her work includes *Lonely Face* by Yeng Pway Ngon, *Bloodline* by Patigül, *Lake Like a Mirror* by Ho Sok Fong, and *Mystery Train* by Can Xue. Her translation of Dorothy Tse's poem 'Cloth Birds' was a winner of the 2019 Words Without Borders Poems in Translation Prize. After several years in Hong Kong, she now lives in Amsterdam.

The text of *Owlish* is set in Adobe Jenson Pro.
Book design by Rachel Holscher.
Composition by Bookmobile Design & Digital
Publisher Services, Minneapolis, Minnesota.

100 percent postconsumer wastepaper.